"Had your fill yet?" he fro

"Not just yet," she chuckle

his form one last time, "But you *do* seem to be in something of a hurry. Maybe later I'll let you tie me to the train tracks, eh Snidely?"

"Enough stalling!" He growled, his fists clenching at his sides, "One way or the other you're coming with me, and. I don't want to have to hit you," he narrowed his eyes, "So don't make me have to!"

Her smile widened and she licked a fang, continuing to undress him with her purple eyes, "Oh you *are* kinky! I only hope you hit better than your friend throws!" She frowned, wondering where the source of the red aura had gone to. Not wanting to break her composure, she forced a coy smirk and wagged her hips, "Now, if you'll excuse me"—she smirked and turned her back to him—"I was just about to catch my dinner."

She felt his icy gaze chill her back and his heavy boots followed, daring her to continue. She rolled her eyes and turned back, lunging at him.

"Enough of this!"

"Wai—"

His speech and his advance ceased as he was taken off guard and she took the opportunity to jump up and shoved both of her high-heeled boots into his chest, rocketing him off the balcony and sending him crashing into a nearby willow tree.

She landed with cat-like grace on her feet and began a cocky swagger towards and then past him. His mismatched and bewildered eyes followed her, taking in her teasing wink as she disappeared.

"Dinner time!" She purred.

The city was still several miles south of the cabin she was staying at—or, rather, *had* been staying at. Now that she'd been found by *someone* that wanted her she'd have to find a new home.

She sighed, "On the road again…" She shook her head as the vampire's shocked face bobbed into her mind. "That bastard!"

"You hurt him pretty bad, you know," Devon chided her.

"So you finally decided to come out, huh?" She smiled, not bothering to glance over at her ghostly companion.

The warmth—an ever-constant reminder of his presence—wrapped around her. She exhaled, enjoying the otherworldly embrace for only a moment before looking over at him. Even as a ghost, he retained his beautiful looks; an eternal mirror of how he was—thankfully—before the accident. He smiled warmly at her. Despite everything she'd done to him, he was still so kind to her.

And that hurt more than he knew.

"I'll find a body for you, Devon. I promise," she said, biting her lip.

"That's not what I said," his voice hardened.

She nodded, "I know what you said. Doesn't change the fact that I'm going to find you a body."

She had been looking—always had been—but, whenever she found a suitable human body, Devon would always stop their impending deaths and discourage her at the last minute.

"Serena, you know how I feel about that," Devon said.

She ignored his words. Nothing he'd said or ever could say would sway her. She wanted to feel him again; be able to enjoy his physical embrace and not just some warm air. He was, and always would be, the only one for her. Hell, she'd give up drinking blood and start gagging down that synthetic crap if he asked her to. He was the only one to see her as her true self because she refused to show it to any other.

"Devon, I want to be with you again," she finally said, stifling her approaching tears before they could spill down her cheeks. She wouldn't let him see her cry. She knew how much that hurt him. "To *really* be with you!"

She paused beside a sapling and enjoyed a cool summer night's breeze as it wrapped around her, teasing her senses as it mingled with Devon's warmth.

4

Colleen
Thanks for reading
& I hope you
enjoy.
Missed ya
at the
Con!

MEGAN J. PARKER

Scarlet Night

This is a work of fiction. Names, characters places, and incidents either are the product of the author's imagination or are used fictitiously. Any resemblance to actual persons living or dead, events, or locales is entirely coincidental.

Dedicated to the strong heroine or hero in you!

ACKNOWLEDGEMENTS

After a rather exciting year of founding Tiger Dynasty Publishing and getting both Nathan Squiers (my wonderful fiancé) and my pieces along with our other authors published, I am very happy to see "Scarlet Night" back up in publication. However, I'd like to shout out to everyone who has supported me in my writing and the tremendous efforts others have put forth in either just leaving me a review, or sharing my work on several pages.

First off, I'd like to thank Jenny Bynum, an amazing supporter in the indie community. She puts forth such an effort in order to help indie authors grow in the community. Secondly, I want to give a shout out to Danael McGuire! Danael, without your amazing organization and planning, Tiger Dynasty would be lost. Also for always having an open ear when I needed it and willing to beta anything of mine! No matter the difficulty, you are always there to lend a hand! Last, but not least, I'd like to thank Nathan Squiers for making me dream a possibility. Without his dedication and attention to details and editing, Scarlet Night would not be what it is now. You are the best fellow author and fiancé ever! These past ten years have been incredible with you!

And then there's one more important individual here...YOU! I wouldn't be anywhere without my readers. So, thank you!

Xoxo
Megan J. Parker

"LOVE IS A SPIRIT ALL COMPACT OF FIRE"
-WILLIAM SHAKESPEARE

CHAPTER ONE
A SCARLET NIGHT

SENSING A POWERFUL ENERGY source approaching, Serena opened the door and stepped out of her cabin and onto the front porch. She stood, scanning through the blackness beyond the trees in an effort to locate the source. A snapping branch sounded to the left and she turned her head towards it right before a flash of light to the right snapped her attention back.

"SHIT!"

She shifted on her heels, bracing herself as the bright red blast shot at her and lifted her hands out of reflex. Though the approaching wave was fast, she had more than enough time to throw her aura in front of her in a defensive orb. As the scarlet wave collided with her shimmering purple shield, a violent flash of light illuminated the woods and everything in it.

Except the source of the attack…

Cursing under her breath, Serena jumped from the porch; her aura poised to defend against another attack, and started in the direction of her unwelcome guest. As she crossed the threshold dividing the clearing from the dense forest, she felt a spike of energy and saw a dark blue aura swirl in the distance.

"Stop right there!" a deep male voice called out past the glow.

"Oh? And why should I do that?" Serena asked, doing nothing to mask her snide tone. As the sound of heavy boots on the forest floor advanced, her lip curled at the familiar energy, and she let her aura whip out and tear a portion of a nearby tree trunk as a warning, "Leave now, mister mystery-vamp!"

The intruder growled at her hostility, and the blue aura coiled and spiked with his aggravation. "No! You're coming with me!" Then, as an afterthought, "… Serena."

"You sound pretty confident there," she mocked, smiling and licking her parched lips as the smell of fresh blood wafted from the stranger, "Tell me, have you fed from a human? You *know* that's a criminal offense, right?" She smirked, "Wouldn't want to see you fall on the wrong side of our kind's law."

"I *am* our kind's law!" a roar bellowed from his chest, "And I don't answer YOUR questions!"

He took one final step towards her, and she fought her body's urge to swoon. He was *gorgeous!* His skin, now lit under the glow of the moon, seemed to break through his inky mane, which spilled onto his shoulders. Over his brow was a sharply-contrasting streak of silver hair—like a sliver of moonlight in an otherwise dark sky—that hung over his forehead and between his piercing gaze.

His gaze…

Each of his eyes was unique; a bright and piercing blue on his left and a ghostly pale right that shimmered like a pearl. She smirked as his aura spiked impatiently as she continued to take in the sight.

2

Devon's unwavering warmth...

No matter what, she knew that he would always be there for her. Not even the fire could stop him from finding his way back to her three years earlier. She looked down and shook her head.

She wanted to fix it...

She wanted to stop it!

Waves of intense heat pushed her back; pushed her away from him. Still down on one knee, Devon was unable to move fast enough to save them both. The hollow, echoing taunt of his offered ring hitting the floor chilled her heart as he stood and planted himself protectively in front of her.

"Serena, I love you, always."

His last words, spoken moments before the fire had started, were already growing cold with grief as he'd used the last of his strength to push her into the tugging hold of the fleeing crowd. There was no pulling free from the combined force of the group as they unknowingly dragged her out of the ballroom, crying and screaming as the roof collapsed behind her, taking her happiness with it.

She blinked, still feeling the phantom flames burn through the fabric of time, and wiped away the tears. She couldn't stop them that time around. Not that she wouldn't have tried, but it was useless. When the memory surfaced, her awareness sank. Devon's aura, knowing and sympathetic, was already wrapped tightly around her. And though it was comforting, it wasn't enough for her.

Approaching footsteps sounded from the clearing and instinctively brought out the fighter in her, the trails of tears drying up on cue.

There, standing and watching her with those wonderfully mismatched eyes, was her attacker.

Though his face didn't show it, his slouched body, weighed down with agony, was in so much pain that it hurt her to see him. Frowning, she looked away, realizing then just how much damage she'd inflicted.

"What do you want?" She made no move to fight, having no strength or desire to do so.

He stayed quiet for a moment and the breeze from earlier came back, colder than before. She frowned at the sudden chill;

Devon and his warmth had disappeared, leaving her alone with the vampire.

"I-I… n-need you to come with me," his voice cracked, and, though Serena wanted to believe it was from the pain she'd dealt him, she could see that it was something else.

Something darker.

For a moment he was silent as he worked to steady his labored breathing. Then, as the tension in his body melted away, he locked his mismatched eyes on her. "You need to come with me," he said, "You'll be safe."

Despite the confusion she felt from his words—and from the unnerving growl in his voice that carried them—she was surprised to find that she believed him.

Against every instinct she'd ever learned, she stepped towards him, still staring into his eyes.

More than anything else she needed Devon. But, feeling a whole new type of warmth emanating from those eyes, she realized that she needed something else.

Something more than just warmth.

"Serena," the mystery vampire called to her, his voice no longer his own. She took another step, driven by that voice and the promises behind it, something in that voice made her want it all the more. "Serena!" he called again, the tone and pitch cutting through the haze of arousal and startling her with the now-obvious truth.

She faltered, nearly collapsing, and stared with wide eyes at the suddenly rigid vampire.

"Devon?"

The vampire's face twisted for a moment, experimenting with its own expressions before settling with a wide smile and nodding.

"But… how?" she stammered, still staring.

"His guard was down," he explained, "The gate was open so I… I just took it. I don't know how long I'll be able to hold it, but for now…" He bit his lip and blushed; his flood of emotions assaulting his stolen body's cheeks.

Stolen or not, she rushed to him, wrapping her arms tightly

around the broad back of the stranger that now housed her lover. Despite everything, with her eyes clenched and buried in the body's chest, she could feel him there.

Her Devon!

Even in a different body, it still felt right.

Large hands met her face and lifted her chin, a flood of his classic warmth and that of the new body's natural heat seeped into her as he brushed her cheeks and she closed her eyes to savor the feeling. Devon lifted her face further towards him and pressed his new lips to hers. Ignoring the subtle differences, she wrapped her arms tightly around his neck, turning the kiss from an exploration to a fierce, passion-filled attack.

She'd been so damn starved for it that the first taste had awakened a hunger she'd long since forgotten.

She forgot how to breath then, but soon found it as he trailed kisses down her chin and a desperate gasp ripped from her burning lungs. Lips still wet with their combined moisture brushed down her neck. Another gasp seeped out, reaching a peak as his tongue ran across her collarbone.

Her senses grew more receptive to everything as their auras collided and mingled, creating a bright and pulsating wave of multicolored light that expanded and contracted rhythmically around them. Devon eased her to the forest floor, the gentle-yet-firm hold the same as she'd remembered it. He pulled away then, beginning to peel the shirt from his borrowed torso, and she reached out to trail her fingertips across the strong, tattoo-covered chest as it emerged. She wanted to reach past the flesh and into Devon, feel everything with him. Even after all those celibate years their passion proved strong, and she was willing to look past the flesh to once again experience who they had been when they had become one.

He began to explore her body all over again, clearly reminding himself of the dips and curves he had not traveled in so long, and she gasped and arched against the static shocks that lit up her nerve endings with each inch he took. Pressing his every essence into her, they once again became one.

Serena explored the new body, rubbing her hands across his entire being as he continued the dance above. The bliss was too much for her and soon her climax reached. As the sounds of her cries filled the forest she felt his body release as well, together finally.

As their bodies entangled on the forest floor, their cries sounded together as they climbed their way to pure ecstasy.

"WHAT THE HELL?"

Serena blinked at the outburst, shaking the sleep from her system as she sat up in a daze. For a moment she was reminded of the previous night as the body heat from her partner's naked body seeped into her own. Then, as her eyes finally met his mismatched own, she was thrown off of him and onto the dew-coated grass. She cried out as the chilled moisture assaulted her bare skin.

"Ow! You asshole!" She glared, trying to ignore the burning of her cheeks as she realized her situation.

"What did you drug me with?" he jumped to his feet and began snatching up the clothes that lay scattered all over the clearing and throwing what didn't belong to him in her direction. "God dammit," he snarled, yanking his pants up, "Where the hell is my belt?"

"Probably in the tree where you threw it last night, you dick!" Serena retrieved her clothes and began to slip into them, keeping her eyes on his chest and the large tribal designs and fresh scratches littered about thereon. Only when his glare returned with laser-focus on her did she avert her gaze, "And for the record, I did NOT drug you!"

He glanced skyward, his shoulders sagging as he spotted the length of leather dangling from a branch. Trying to remain intimidating, he hid his growing sense of defeat, failing to control his aura's all-too-clear reaction. "Then why, pray-tell, am I waking up NAKED with you? Why can't I remember anything from last night?"

Serena clucked her tongue, unsure of how to explain the situation without sounding like part of a strange, ghostly date-raping.

"Look, call me 'old fashioned', but I make it an effort to *remember* how I come to be naked with somebody!" He gave up on retrieving his belt and ducked into his jacket, a growl emerging from his throat.

"Oh? I'm so goddam sorry to have interfered with your obviously detailed and intimate list of skanks and whores," she countered, "I'm sure it's very confusing to wake up in this sort of a situation and not have to PAY your partner!"

"You bitch," he bared his fangs, "I can guarantee that they're a better lay than you could ever hope to be!"

Serena's breath caught in her throat at that and she bit her lip, looking down.

He paused, his enraged features softening as he took in her reaction. After a silent moment, he cleared his throat and calmed his tone, "So, did we…?"

"We…" Serena blushed and dared a glance at him, seeing his confusion and understanding his apprehension. She nodded once, "Yes. We did."

"Dammit!" He rubbed the back of his neck and turned away from her, "This was not supposed to happen!"

"I… I'm sorry. If it makes you feel any better, it wasn't exactly planned," the sincerity felt strange to Serena, "I mean, I don't even know your name!" A morning breeze began to pick up and the vampire looked over to meet her apologetic gaze; a gaze she had a hard time maintaining. She had no right to blame him for his reaction. There she stood, still *smelling* like him and not even *knowing* his name!

"Zane," he said with a sigh.

Her eyes shifted back towards him, "Wh-what?"

"Zane; it's my name. Zane Murdoch," he nodded to himself as

his aura shifted at the mention of his name. "It's only right that you know that much," he scowled at her confusion before suddenly looking away. Narrowing his eyes, he growled and glanced towards the shadowed depths of the forest.

"What?" Serena stepped forward to join him at his side, "What is it?"

Zane's aura tightened and coiled like a serpent, "We're not alone."

Serena turned in the direction of his gaze and squinted against the rising sun, "I don't see any—"

"DOWN!"

Zane pivoted on his heel as he threw his arm out, taking Serena by surprise as he caught her across the chest and pulled her down as a flash of muscle and teeth shot over their heads.

"What the fuck?" Serena felt her body shake with a flood of adrenaline.

Looking up, she spotted the four therions—already shifted into their bestial bodies and snarling through dripping fangs—as they regrouped in the clearing and prepared for a second pass at them.

Zane solidified his stance and bared his fangs. "STAND DOWN OR I *WILL* EXECUTE ALL OF YOU!"

The four snarling beasts didn't falter; didn't even respond—not even on an auric level—to the threat.

Serena rolled her eyes, "Maybe you should flash a badge or something."

"Shut up and keep your guard up!" Zane growled, his eyes narrowing and his body shaking with rage as the familiar energy flared up.

Serena stared for a moment as his tattoos began to glow brighter and brighter, mirroring his rapidly growing rage.

"Uh... Right," she nodded, solidifying her own stance despite the flood of new questions her strange comrade was earning with each passing second. With the therions closing in, she clenched her fists and focused her aura.

The nearest of the attacking shapeshifters focused on Zane and pounced, leading with its massive claws and coming down in a vicious arc with its unnaturally large fangs gaping and snapping hungrily in anticipation of his flesh. Serena gaped as Zane hissed—baring his fangs as his face started to warp and shift and his tattoos glowed brighter—and pulled back his hand. As Serena watched, Zane elongated and locked his fingers like the tip of a blade and drove it into his attacker's throat. As the beast's momentum forced it downward, Zane's hand sank deeper and deeper into its body and Serena watched in horrified awe as it collapsed to the ground with her ally's arm buried inside it to his elbow. Slowly and methodically Zane withdrew his hand and tore the fallen therion's still-beating heart through its chest and back out through the wound. Appalled by his own prize, he threw the organ to the ground and brought his boot down on it. Still convulsing and writhing in pain, the therion collapsed at that moment, finally dead. Seeing the ease with which Zane dispatched of their comrade, the others thought better of their plans and turned to flee.

"N-not... getting off that eas—ahh! Fuck! *Fuck*!" Zane roared, his voice growing deep and gravelly as the tattoos continued to glow. In the blink of an eye, he'd crossed the distance between them and cut off the remaining therions, easily ripping the head off of one as he lifted his hand in the direction of the other two and wrapping his aura—as it shifted unnaturally from blue to red; the *same* aura from the night before!—around them and pulling them off their feet. In the grip of Zane's inexplicable power, the two whimpered and writhed before the last of their life was choked from them, and he cast their corpses aside like toys.

Though the four were already dead, his body continued to convulse and twitch as he dropped to his knees, clutching his head and whimpering in obvious agony. Though worried, her concern for what was happening held her back; the mystery of what was happening to him—what he was *becoming*—too terrifying to approach.

After a moment his aura began to deflate and turned back to

blue, and she dared the first step towards him. As she drew nearer, he looked up with exhausted eyes.

"What did you... Y-your aura! It—it changed! Then the other aura... That was *just* you last night?" she shook her head, still not believing what she'd just witnessed, "H-how were you able to do that?"

Zane looked over, his mismatched eyes shimmering brighter than ever before as he struggled to even his heaving breaths, "I... I'm not what you think I am."

CHAPTER TWO
FLASHBACK

"OKAY! I'LL BITE, MISTER WIZARD! IF you're not what I *think* you are, then just what the hell *are* you?" Serena asked as she followed Zane through the forest towards the city.

"A monster, but that's not really important right now," Zane answered quickly.

Serena sighed, "Well *that's* eerie and ominous. You should probably consider taking Prozac or something; all that self-loathing stuff ain't doing it for me."

"Guess it's a good thing I'm not doing it for you then, ain't it?"

Then, obviously wanting to change the subject: "I was sent to find you"—he looked over his shoulder at her with cold eyes—"by your father."

"Wait! My *father* sent you?" she stopped and sneered, shaking her head, "Some nerve that asshole has to send one of his jerk-off lackeys out here to try and get me to come back to the clan! Screw that... and screw you!" Serena pivoted on one heel and started back towards her cabin, "Tell the old man to go die and rot in he—"

"He *is* dead!" Zane's voice was low and even, but there was more than enough venom and malice in those two words to sink into Serena's heart.

Though she was sure he'd seen the shift in her posture at the news, she kept her back turned. "I don't care," she lied, hoping it sounded convincing enough, "Do you think that's going to make a difference?" she cried out, the feeling of guilt piled in her stomach even as she spoke the words.

Zane stepped in front of her as she started to storm off again, his body shaking as though he were having some sort of seizure. Eyes widening in surprise, Serena backed away, noticing that the complex designs of his tattoos had begun to glow red.

"Listen to me! Your father *died* protecting you and everything—everyone!—he cares about! And he entrusted *me* with the task of getting your spoiled ass back in the clan's walls! You will take your place where you've always belonged or you'll let down a shit-load of fellow clan members who are depending on you!"

Serena froze as the thought that she might have even been important to the clan slapped her in the face. Looking up at Zane, she realized how close he must have been to her father. She frowned, seeing the glowing designs on his neck begin to fade as he began to rub at them; remembering how the tattoos had reacted when Devon had taken over. She tilted her head and studied him for a moment.

"Your tattoos...?" Though she was trying to steer the conversation away from something that was clearly upsetting him,

her curiosity about him was too great to shift entirely. And, even if
it was only somewhat, she was still concerned by the pained look
on his face. Though it *was* only somewhat. She sighed and shook
her head. She didn't need all this new chaos.

"DON'T!"—He frowned, averting his enraged gaze from her
worried one—"Just... don't worry about them. They're nothing
important to the situation. Right now we have a lot more to talk
about." As his tone and breathing calmed, the tattoos began to fade
back to their normal hue.

Serena watched the phenomenon, scrutinizing both the tattoos
and their owner. Finally she nodded, letting out a heavy sigh, "I'll
come. It's been a while since I've been around other people. I
guess it might be nice." She smirked, strolling by him, "*Might* be."
After a moment she looked back over to his now-startled
expression and realized that her words had appeared to calm him a
great deal.

Somehow, knowing this made her feel at peace.

They reached the clan's headquarters faster than Serena was
ready for and she found herself frozen at the entrance, staring at
the once-familiar surroundings with a growing sense of nostalgia
and dread. The entrance still seemed like nothing more than a
normal parking garage entrance, and to any human walking by it
would appear to be just another office building standing amongst
many others like it. That, however, was *exactly* how the Clan of Vail
and its members wanted it.

Though she could've easily stood and stared at the immense
parking garage for several hours more without beginning to fathom
what lay beyond, Zane's patience wasn't committed to such
indulgences and a firm grip pulled her forward. Stumbling to keep
up with the warrior's well-trained pace, they entered the service
elevator at the other end of the corridor.

As the doors slid shut behind them, a wave of claustrophobia knocked the air from Serena's chest and she gasped in a panic.

"Stop it! You're fine!" Zane said, sounding more annoyed than assuring as he flipped open a panel near the row of buttons. His fingers moved rhythmically over the hidden dial, and as he entered a final keystroke a mechanical chime sounded and the buttons shifted from yellow to red.

Still trying to get control of her nerves, Serena stared as her escort stabbed his calloused thumb onto one of the now-scarlet levels and there was a jolt as they began to descend.

"Th-that's… that's new," she inhaled deeply and tried to let it out slow to ease any future stutters.

"Yes," Zane nodded, standing ramrod straight and staring blankly at the doors, "Your father felt the need to boost security due to some recent incidents."

Serena bit her lip, "Does this have something to do with what happened to the Odin Cla—"

"It has something to do with *many* things that your father felt deserved his attention," his gaze shifted towards her and he shook his head slightly.

"I see…" Serena looked down and wondered to herself what else she had missed.

As the elevator slowed and stopped, the two doors opened to reveal the headquarters' main lobby, Zane showed no hesitation in stepping past into the room. Serena again found herself frozen at the familiar-yet-foreign scene. Realizing that he had exited alone, he turned and stared expectantly at her, signaling with his eyes for her to follow. Though her pride was quickly beginning to fracture, she couldn't shake the familiar and crippling feeling.

A feeling like…

Just go, Serena! Devon's voice echoed in her mind and enveloped her in his warmth. She sighed, glancing over at Devon's ghostly silhouette for one last nod of support before turning to Zane, who was staring impatiently at her.

She finally nodded and stepped out of the elevator.

The subterranean complex was as massive as she'd

remembered. As the elevator doors slid shut with a soft hum behind her, she accepted with only a minor tremor of panic that she *was* underground. Despite this, her father and his efforts had transformed their headquarters into something befitting royalty, and she was reminded of this fact as she caught sight of a large marble fountain a short distance away. A series of colored lights surrounded and adorned the monument, lending a sense of beauty and serenity to the otherwise barren setting. Past this, the room forked off into several corridors where the clan member's rooms were kept.

Despite her father's eye for décor, it was all still the same.

Serena couldn't help but smile at the wave of nostalgia that flooded her at the sight of her childhood home. Though she couldn't honestly say that they'd *all* been good, it was still the site of many fond childhood memories. As a little girl, she had always thought of the clan's headquarters as her own, personal five-star resort, and as she welcomed the various flashbacks she stepped towards the fountain. Despite the rush of emotions, the rhythmic and serene sound of flowing water over the intricately carved marble had a soothing effect and she casually ran the tips of her fingers across the surface and watched the ripples echo out from her touch.

When she was young; she had always been fascinated with the fountains in the park and had often asked to go out to see them. However, due to the dangers that came with being both a part of such an influential clan *and* the daughter of its leader, casual outings of any kind were few and far between.

"He said it was built for you," Zane stepped over, his purposeful stride resounding on the tile floor, and pulled Serena from her own mind. "He never said too much concerning it, but we all knew. I used to find him sitting here when things were quiet enough and he thought he was alone."

"My father… did this… for me?" She pulled her fingers away from the water and hurried to rub away a burning pool that had begun to well in her eye, "I wouldn't've thought, after everything that had happened that he'd even *want* to remember me." Zane shrugged and sat on the outer edge of the fountain's foundation. Letting out a sigh, he leaned forward, resting his elbows on his knees, suddenly looking very exhausted. He stayed quiet, keeping his gaze locked on the floor as Serena finished her thoughts, and, while she appreciated it, it wasn't a comfortable situation to be in with company. Dragging her focus away from the fountain, she turned her back to it and sat next to Zane. "How did you and he meet anyway?"

The question forced a smile to his otherwise sullen face and he rubbed absently at the back of his neck. "It's a *long* fuckin' story…" He chuckled and shook his head, "I guess you could say he adopted me," he scoffed at his own choice of words and shook his head. For the first time since their meeting, Serena saw Zane offer a genuine smile. "Your fathe—"

"There you are! I was starting to worry you'd skipped town, Zane!" an excited, warm voice chimed from behind. Zane let out a small growl and cupped his face in his hands, beginning to grumble incoherently into his palms, as the source's soft footsteps plodded towards them. "Is this her? Did you *really* find her *that* fast?"

Zane grumbled and pulled his face from his palms, "No, Zoey. This is a *hooker* that I wanted to hire for our warriors! Perhaps leap out of a cake and—"

"Oh stop! Like you'd *ever* get something *this* classy! I'd recognize the fruits of Gregori's lively aura *any*where!" The spritely girl hopped in front of them, her short, cartoon-like blue hair bobbing and swaying as she traded glances from her equally-blue eyes between the two. "I can't believe it! You're *really* here!" She clapped excitedly, and Serena blushed and chuckled nervously. She wasn't normally one to be put off guard, but this girl was so damn chipper. After another moment of giddy bouncing, she smirked over at Zane, who had retreated back into the comfort of his palms to continue his grumbling, "Aw! Poor Zaney, are we still cranky about being scolded earlier? I thought you were all better." Serena didn't pretend to understand what she meant, but knew from

Zane's reaction that there was no point in questioning it at that point. "So"—she shifted her shimmering eyes back to her—"*this* is Gregori's daughter! Wow! She looks just like Rose! Did you know you look *just* like your mother?"

Serena felt a twitch in her eye at the mention of her mother.

Zane frowned and shook his head at her, "Zoey, that isn't really a—"

"Oh hush!" Zoey stuck out her tongue at him, "You've seen the pictures, too! You can't deny it! You and I have *both* heard all his stories!"

Zane growled and looked away, not offering a response. Serena watched him for a moment, wondering what he was thinking, before turning to Zoey.

"How do you know so much about me?" Serena asked, not trying to hide the venom in her tone. She'd noticed instantly that she had no aura surrounding her petite body, which meant she was either an auric vampire or a corpse, and she was far too lively for the latter. And, though aurics *did* have the ability to read minds, she hadn't felt the familiar tug of an invading presence in her head. Had she been able to sneak into her head when her guard was down?

Zoey's exuberant smile remained as she shook her head, "No need to worry! Your father just told me a lot about you and your mother. He spoke very highly of you."

Serena frowned, "Are you one of the clan's warriors?"

Zoey shrugged, "More or less. I can get a job done when I need to, but your father was more interested in my research."

"What kind of research?" Serena cocked an eyebrow.

"Hematology, magic, and microbiological development," she giggled as two sets of eyes went glassy, "Blood. I make blood. Well, *fake* blood; fake, *enchanted* blood. Zane, do you remember when The Gamer wa—"

Zane groaned, "Zoey. Babbling!"

"Oh, right. Sorry," she giggled again. "Anyway, your father was interested in a synthetic blood substitute with nearly *ten*-times the potency."

"Don't mind her," Zane rolled his eyes, "Zoey gets chatty when she's nervous."

Zoey pouted and stuck her tongue out at him again.

Serena sighed again and looked over at the two. They both were so welcoming to her. Well, Zoey was at least; Zane didn't seem like he cared much one way or the other. She looked down and tugged at her skirt a bit, remembering their night together.

"You still with us, Princess?" Zane narrowed his gaze at her, his eyes burning into her, "Now that you're here, we can't have you slipping off into la-la land at your leisure."

She frowned, again questioning just *what* he was and wondering if he had actually read her thoughts or if he was just perceptive.

"You see that, Zane? You *scare* the poor girl! She's already been through a lot, so why don't you give her a break?" Zoey smiled warmly and turned to her, "Serena, would you care to go for a walk with me?"

"Not now! She needs to be caught up on what she's missed!" Zane said as he went to step between them.

Serena's eyes narrowed and she pulled back her lip. She *hated* to be answered for! "No, Zane,"—she spat out his name like a bad taste—"I think what I *need* is to go for a walk." Serena shot him a look and started forward, walking around him and linking her arm with Zoey's as she pulled them both towards the exit.

"We can do it another time if it's a problem…" Zoey whispered as Serena continued forward. Though she was reluctant to follow with Zane's scorching gaze burning into their backs, she was unable to counter Serena's determination and strength and was forced through the doors.

"It's okay! No time like the present, right? Besides look at his face! It's priceless!" Serena smirked and turned back for a moment to shoot Zane a wink and cackle as his eyes narrowed and he clenched his fists.

"I'm not sure Zane is going to like this…" Zoey chewed on her lip, but continued forward from Serena's pull.

"Oh, he's all bark and no bite!" Serena laughed.

Zoey whimpered, "I wish that were true…"

"Just come back soon!" Zane's growling voice echoed after them, followed shortly after by the sound of his heavy steps as he stomped off.

"Oh! You're burned!" Zoey frowned as she spotted the irritated red patch on Serena's back.

They had found their way to a small spot in the forest near the city and sat by a log that gave them a wonderful view of a small pond glowing in the moonlight. Serena sighed, knowing she could easily make it back to her cabin from this distance.

So close to her serenity and solitude with Devon…

"It's from earlier. I fell asleep in the forest and woke up in the sun. It's really not as bad as it looks," she explained, trying to shift her top to cover the spot—hoping she wouldn't reveal any details about the night before. Though Zane was already upset about the whole thing, he would probably only get angrier if Zoey found out. She smirked at the thought and played with the idea a moment longer.

"Oh! Come to think of it, Zane did seem more agitated than normal! The sun's always done a number on him because of his curse and all," Zoey bit her lip and turned her attention towards some nearby flowers.

"Curse?" Serena's eyes widened and she leaned forward, "What do you mean? Just what's his problem anyway?"

"That's… not really my story to tell," Zoey shook her head and quickly stood, heading off into the woods. "I'll be right back. I'm going to see if I can't find something that might help your burn. Stay here."

Before Serena could respond she had rushed into the forest, disappearing into the thick blackness of the trees.

Serena shivered and looked up into the moonlight. Who—or,

more to the point, *what*—was Zane really?

Should I be nervous? Devon's voice called to her as his auric visage materialized in front of her, *You know that you've been thinking about him an awful lot lately, right?*

"Not like *that*!" Serena lashed out defensively before reigning in her emotions. She shook her head, more to herself than to Devon, "I guess it's... it's just that I'm having a hard time trusting him and all. Plus, it's hard to imagine rejoining my father's clan after..."

There's something about him; some strange power. I've never seen anything like it before, but when I possessed him there was... something else inside. Devon continued, concern weaving through his voice as he struggled to explain.

"You don't have to worry about me. I know better than to let my guard down, especially not for some douchebag I just met," she sighed and looked into the water.

Devon stared at her a moment longer before he faded and disappeared from her sight. She knew she had upset him with what she said and she frowned as the loneliness crept up on her.

Where had Zoey gone off to?

Zoey hummed softly as she walked into an opening in the forest and kneeled down, absently examining the plants for any that might help with Serena's burn. Though she *was* concerned, the excursion was more for Zane and his secret. She sighed, continuing to ruffle through the various plants, considering heading back before the sound of a violin resonated through the area and she looked up to find the source. Though eerie and out of place, the music was both beautiful and heart-wrenching. She stepped towards the direction and began to follow the sound.

Peeking through the trees, she saw a tall, lean man perched against a tree with an empty bottle of vodka lying beside him. The music, she realized, was coming from him, and she watched, entranced, as he played an old, beat-up violin that seemed to be held together solely by the tenderness that its owner played it with. She stared at him for a time, taking in his handsome features. Dark-brown hair, long and unkempt, poured over his head and down to his shoulders; a great deal of the wild mane covering his face as he played. Past the curtain of hair, however, Zoey could make out his fierce eyes—dark and partially hidden behind hair and shadow—as they stared at the neck of the instrument and filled with an animal ferocity. Without meaning to, she felt herself stepping forward. She could see that he was a theriomorph—the shape-shifters responsible for almost every werewolf legend ever told—and a strong one, at that. His dark-green aura writhed and throbbed with a bestial fury and she could sense the raw energy radiating from him as he played. And while the code of ethics for the Clan of Vail would have her see *any* therion as an enemy, she couldn't bring herself to fear or hate him. Though, Zoey didn't mind therions as much as the others in her clan, they *were* still an enemy, and with the clan's recent trauma still weakening their fortitude she knew it wouldn't take much to collapse the system by breaking rules. Still, enemy or not, this particular therion didn't seem to be engaged in anything to warrant an attack and, since the clan *was* bound to The Council's laws, she saw no reason to attack.

So lost in her own thoughts, Zoey hadn't realized the music stopped when her presence had been discovered.

"Who are you?" he growled, his voice as smooth and deep as an angry ocean wave.

She stifled a shiver as it crept down her spine and went to turn away as fast as she had come. This was a mistake! The last thing she or the clan needed was a situation with a therion pack.

"Don't think so!" She turned to see him barreling towards her, his speed catching her off guard. The calm grace and pacing that he'd applied to his music were gone, replaced by a blur of predatory intent.

His hand clamped down on her wrist like a wolf's jaws and she cried out as she was yanked back. His hand could've easily crushed her entire arm if he was inclined to do so, and the only thing she could do was turn and look back at him. Her eyes locked on to his and she gulped to swallow her encroaching gasp. He was marvelous. Even more so up close than she could've imagined. His eyes were not black, but a deep greenish-brown with specs of gold in them that shimmered with the excitement of new prey and, despite *being* that prey, made her shiver to her core. His face, once calm and reflective on his art, was now drawn tight with the fury and confidence of a killer. She couldn't stop staring at his beauty and felt herself aware of things she had never before felt. She felt his arm hesitate as well around her wrist. She shook her head quickly, realizing she was ogling.

"Are you done yet?" he asked as a growl emitted from deep within his chest.

"I'm sorry! I didn't mean to stare," she finally found her voice—though cracked and shrill—and tried to plead her case. Though there wasn't much of a case to plea; they both knew she had meant to stare and that she wasn't sorry for it, either.

Baring his, thankfully, still-human teeth at her, he leaned over and sniffed at her throat. Her breath caught and she held back the urge to cough as the proximity to her windpipe was invaded. Then, with the speed and grace she'd come to expect in such a short time of knowing him, he drew back and snarled. "You're with *them*! Vail! You reek of their clan!" he bellowed as he grabbed her by her throat with his other hand and began to squeeze. "Spying on me? Hoping to plan an attack on my pack, eh?" She could smell the alcohol radiating off him and her sea-blue aura began to whip out in an effort to escape. His speed and strength were too great, however, and as his choking grip continued to hold the air from her lungs her head began spinning. With a hazy sense of direction and a fading recollection of her training swimming lazily in her oxygen-starved brain, her auric tendrils quickly died and fell limply before withdrawing back into her body.

"L-Let go!" She gasped, struggling to get the words out, "Won't...hu-urt!" She cried out, the pain seizing her and her voice came out as a soft squeak. She was going to die! Unable to calm her fading mind to focus her aura, her frail body thrashed and clawed in an effort to free itself from the vice around her throat.

But it only made him squeeze that much harder.

"Pretty thing like you, huh? Did they send you? Did you think you could seduce me and gain my trust? Maybe even allow you into my pack for a fuck?" he growled, his hold loosening only a bit as his eyes moved to her chest.

She whimpered as her body began to shake even more. She couldn't die, not yet.

He brought his free hand up and traced a growing claw down her neck and onto her chest as he let out a groan. Zoey's body had stopped shaking and she let out a soft breath as his grasp loosened even more.

He rubbed at his temple with his free hand and blinked his eyes several times, "Dammit. Shouldn't have drank so much..." He growled and shook his head, looking up at her and his eyes seemed to soften and he began to lower her to the ground. "I... I'm not goi—GAH!"

He cried out and stumbled forward as a bright purple light flashed and collided with his back. Zoey, free of the grip, hit the ground hard with a pained grunt and looked up through her still-unfocused eyes to see what had happened. The therion growled, roaring angrily, and pulled himself up, rubbing at the back of his shoulders. Though the auric blast had been enough to knock him over, he didn't appear to be hurt by the attack.

"... the fuck?" he turned and snarled at his attacker.

Serena glared from atop a nearby tree branch, her purple aura outstretched and "held" in her hands like a bow. As she watched, Serena moved to draw back the "string" on her semi-transparent, neon-purple bow and her aura shifted, appearing ready to fire. Though the therion couldn't see the spectacle of her auric weapon, he *did* have the pleasure of watching her go through the motions.

Zoey frowned. She'd never seen an auric wield their aura that way before, and while it was impressive—albeit unconventional—

she had to do something.

"Serena! Stay back!" She shouted, holding out her hands as she stood.

"Don't think so, Zoey! He was going to kill you!" Serena frowned at Zoey disapprovingly before returning her attention to the therion as she dropped from her perch on the tree and landed in an attack stance.

"Enough of this bullshit!" The therion growled and turned away, rushing off deep into the darkness of the forest. Zoey fought the desire to follow him and scolded herself for even thinking about it. She knew he was dangerous, but she couldn't help but feel drawn to him.

"That's right! Run off, you chicken-shit bastard!" Serena shouted after him and went to move forward.

"Serena... please. Don't," Zoey frowned, holding her own throat where his hand had clutched her. His hand had softened before Serena came in and Zoey wondered what he had planned. She shook her head quickly; knowing it was better to forget him and move on.

"God! He really did a number on you! Good thing I came after you, huh? You would've been killed!" Serena walked over, brushing her fingers across Zoey's already bruising neck, "Come on, we should tell Zane."

"No! Don't!" Zoey frowned, panicked, before forcing herself to smile softly, "I mean, he doesn't need any more issues than he's already got. He'd only start to get angry and probably end up breaking something. Besides, you were here to help out and I'm safe now because of that."

Serena frowned and looked over at Zoey. Something told her it was a bad idea not to tell Zane, but Zoey looked so nervous about his involvement. Besides, she'd known Zane longer and probably had a better idea of how to handle him. She sighed and shook her head. "Let's head back now. He might come back with others, so it's not safe to stay here anymore. You really need to be more careful. Also, if you ever need help when I'm around, you can call out with your aura." Serena started to lead the way and frowned when she realized she was giving survival advice to a clan warrior. She bit her lip and shook her head at herself. Though she wasn't used to trying to help others and sticking up for somebody else, she already saw Zoey like something of a younger sister and felt driven to help protect her.

Zoey followed after and smiled warmly at Serena as she wrapped her arm around Serena's. "You're a true friend, you know that?"

Serena rolled her eyes; "friend" was the last thing she wanted to be right now to anyone. Though, she knew that gesture had made her feel wanted, and that, she couldn't deny, had made her happy.

CHAPTER THREE
FREE THE BEAST

ZANE GROWLED AS HE SAT IN HIS room looking over Gregori's old notes. Without meaning to, his right hand fisted in his hair as he glanced through the handwritten documents over and over again; the calculated and meticulous writing of the Vail Clan's old leader only serving to remind him of what they'd lost. This reminder, coupled with Zoey's disappearance with the Vailean girl, was enough to make the raging creature within him shriek and thrash about. Zane shook his head and growled; leave it to a woman he barely even knew to urge the already-begging-to-befreed beast to fight that much harder.

The letters, from what Zane was able to gather from them, had nothing important hidden within them. He growled again, this time hard enough to make his throat hurt. How did Gregori expect him to understand any of this? He continued through the pile of notes and letters and documents; flipping through page after page of Gregori's thoughts and research. But it all might as well have been written in the language of the ancients; none of the words on *any* of the pages held any clues of what they were supposed to do now; what *he* was supposed to do now!

He sighed, looking at the last page in the stack and frowned, chewing roughly on his lip as he toyed with the idea of starting from the beginning all over again and absently letting his torn lip flood his mouth with his own blood. While he wasn't usually one for dramatic self-destruction, the taste of his own blood gave him something to focus on and provided an illusion of nourishment for the time being. And at least it would put a cork on the beast's appetite…

… for now, at least.

Shaking his head, he pulled one of the yellowing pages from the pile and, rubbing a layer of exhaustion and irritation from his vision, began to read once again:

Zane,

As my most trusted and powerful protégé, I'm entrusting you with a most imperative order.

In the event of my demise, I'm leaving control of the clan to my daughter, Serena. While she is brash and untrained, her strengths lie with her intuition and instinct. I need you to nurture these and guide her in the right direction to ensure our survival. Her lack of involvement with the clan's affairs has kept my son silent and hidden, but there is no doubt in my mind that Keith will see this transfer of power as an insult and a challenge. The promise of controlling Vail will surely motivate a response upon the news of my death and he will stop at nothing to find his sister before we do to see whatever plans he has come to fruition.

Be warned: he is cunning and manipulative and will use her and any others he can coax however he sees fit to achieve his goals.

The recent rise in activity from the neighboring therion tribe has me concerned that he's planning something with them and using his authority as a Council member as a means of gaining momentum. His influences with the Mythos government have grown noticeably stronger, and trusted sources have informed me that he's using these influences to his advantage. Needless to say, this is due cause for concern. While nothing would make me happier than to see Keith put down, killing him will motivate a tactical response from our superiors. If The Council sees Vail as an enemy, nothing will stop them from taking us apart and Keith's standing in their ranks will only be strengthened by his claims; he will become a martyr to his own cause and we cannot allow this to happen.

There has never been a time when it was more imperative that you keep your rage under control. Serena will need guidance and Vail will need stability, and, while none are better suited for the task, your steps in this matter will weigh far heavier on the outcome than any you've taken before.

You've come so far and learned so much, and while I commend you on your progress, I see so much more that can be achieved. I apologize if this letter finds you before I can help you reach those achievements, but there is not a single doubt in my mind that the raging curse within you is nowhere near as powerful as your own resolve.

You've never failed to make me proud, and I feel now is the best time to tell you that you've become something of a son in my eyes. It's time you show your brothers and sisters what you've made so very clear *to me.*

> *Deepest sincerities,*
> *Gregori Vailean*

He felt the beast roar from deep inside of him and he grimaced at the internal tremor, clenching his teeth until it had finally passed. As the riot in his head died down, he was reminded of the burning itch in his body as the curse tried to sneak past his defenses; he growled at his own body, rubbing at his forearms in an effort to dispel the sensation. Try as he might, though, he couldn't calm himself, and another violent growl crept from his throat as he shook his head. Gregori *must* have known he was going to die when he wrote that. All formalities set aside—any sense of forethought or planning that Gregori was renowned for *not* being taken into consideration—Zane *knew* that the old vampire wouldn't have dropped this shit on his lap if it hadn't been the right time.

He was *expecting* to die; *expecting*—and, as he could now see, *planning*—how the clan would run without him.

The memory of Gregori's body the night they found him, riddled with magic-laced bullets and decapitated, sent another violent tremor through his body and he howled in rage and pain.

He'd known!

Gregori had *known* his life was in danger!

That steps had to be taken—actions ensured—for when that happened!

And that meant it could have been prevented!

And *that* meant Zane had failed him…

Snarling at the realization, he glared down at the letter and every word that now shrieked accusations in his mind and frantically began tearing it to shreds. With every fury-fueled tear, his claws grew from his rapidly warping fingers that eventually were too gnarled to grip the pieces any longer. As the confetti ribbons of Gregori's dying request rained down on Zane's floor, his body surged forward and he cried out in rage and pain; his own voice already shifting and sounding foreign to him.

"*N-n-nnn*nNO!" he grabbed his head and pressed against his temples, "N-nnot *here!*" He closed his eyes, taking a deep breath as he tried to stop the beast. He couldn't allow it to come out here; not within the clan's walls. Not with all his unsuspecting comrades within range!

For once, the monster seemed to listen and the chaos beneath his flesh stopped trying to rip through the surface.

His tattoos had just shifted back to their black hue when his cell phone began to ring and he snarled at the sudden noise's assault against his still-sensitive hearing and he struggled to suppress the urge to smash the iPhone into a fine powder like he had with so many phones before it. Though he was able to keep from crumbling the device into pieces upon snatching it up, the force *was* enough to start a network of spider web-like cracks that formed along the screen from the force of his grip.

He glanced down at the fragmented caller-ID and forced his eyes to see through the distortion of broken glass and rage to read "*Unknown caller*". Growling again, he slammed a twitching thumb against the "talk" button.

"Who the *fuck* is this?" he roared into the receiver.

The phone was silent for a moment and Zane felt his anger rise with every second he was forced to endure the silence. Finally a cold and calculated voice picked up:

"I'm calling on behalf of my masters to suggest that you and the others of the Vail Clan adhere to the laws of our people, or we *will* be forced to step in and handle the situation. You have failed to follow proper protocol concerning the passing of your leader and if you do not comply with these laws you and your comrades *will* be considered rogues to The Council and persecuted as such. Our records show that Council-member Keith Vailean is Gregori's successor, and we're well aware that no attempt has been made to contact him concerning these matters. I feel it's only fair to warn you that Keith is not known within our ranks as having patience for—"

"You *and* Keith can go fist-fuck yourselves! Our clan—with or without Gregori—is strong enough to deal with you pussy-footed boot-lickers, and we are not about to hand ourselves over to some spoiled scab-eater who was lucky enough to get a seat with The Council! I'm well-aware of Keith's reputation and have been requested by Gregori, *himself,* not to give him control. I have it on good faith that you're *his* leech and *that* means your authority amounts to jack-shit without a unanimous ruling from the other Council chairs! So unless you've got all the signatures from those that matter I suggest you and your leash-holder either silence your empty threats or bring them to our front door and see how long it takes us to rip you to pieces! You tell him that Daddy knew better and those who are loyal to his memory will *not* be going down without a fight!" he screamed, his voice warping into a full growl.

There was a long silence on the other end as his words registered. Finally, the speaker cleared his throat and began to speak with a wavering voice; "I will trust that wiser minds exist amongst you to speak on the clan's behalf. It would be wise to pass along this message to somebody willing to take the situation into greater consideration, lest a great number of your people be forced to suffer solely as a consequence of your arrogance."

The line went dead then and Zane, unable to control himself any longer, snarled and gripped the phone tighter and tighter until it fell from his palm in pieces. He watched as the remains of the device scattered across the floor.

So much for all the anger management Gregori had been putting him through.

But he didn't care about the phone or the cost to replace it and however many more he'd certainly destroy in the future. Only one thing was clear in his mind at that point…

He wanted… no, *needed* a drink.

The walk was torturous for Zane and, having the forethought to do so, he had brought along a bottle of Gregori's old stock to numb the process. While he was sure the origins of the fantastic liquor had Zoey's name written all over it, it had been Gregori who'd introduced him to his private stash—a pantry of unlabeled bottles that his mentor had always referred to as "Spirits for the spiritless"—a pitch-black liquor that reeked of petrol and tasted like a rotting therion's asshole. While the experience of drinking it was nothing short of agonizing and a single shot of the stuff would probably kill a human in seconds, it was the *perfect* thing—hell, the only thing!—to get past a vampire's superhuman system and get them drunk. Chugging down the last drop of the wretched nectar, he felt his face contort as the fire hit his gut and let out a pained-yet-satisfied groan as it started to take effect. Then, throwing it into the nearest trashcan nearby, he reveled in the sound of the shattered glass and the panicked shrieks and bustling of several rats that had been scavenging nearby.

Satisfied that he had enough of a buzz going to make the scene in style, he stumbled into his favorite bar and cursed as the shift in light assaulted his drunken gaze for a moment. He blinked a few times and tried to coax his eyes to adjust faster for him. When he could finally see well-enough to navigate, he worked his way to his favorite stool and motioned to the bartender.

The decrepit German behind the bar glanced wearily at him and shook his head. Zane smirked wickedly. The old man hated him, and if he hadn't before, then the past few visits had definitely done the trick. Though he wasn't sure if he'd try to call the cops on him after the outcome from his last visit, Zane was too invested on drowning his thoughts to consider going somewhere else. As his usual—a pint of the cheapest beer on tap and a shot of the bar's best bourbon—was being set in front of him, the bartender leaned in close enough for Zane to smell the sauerkraut and scotch in his words.

"We aren't in for a problem t'night, are we boy?"

Zane chuckled and shook his head, "You leave that bottle right here where it belongs and I'll be quiet as a fucking mouse, *Mein Fuhrer!*"

The bartender frowned at Zane's choice of words but only gave a gentle nod before setting the nearly-full bottle of premium bourbon in front of him and turning away. "See to it that ye are! I want to be able t' forget yer even here, boy!" then, as a second thought, "And ye'd better be able to *pay* for that, er else I'm pressin' charges fer sure!"

"Yea yea, Adolf! I got more than enough to buy this *and* the rest of your stock! Now get lost!" Zane grunted and rolled his eyes as he grabbed the bottle of A.H. Hirsch Reserve in his left hand as he downed the pint of Red Dog in a single gulp with his right. When he was certain the old man wasn't looking he reached into his jacket and pulled out a small vial of concentrated "spiritless" that he'd snatched from Gregori's stash and dumped the contents into the bourbon.

Giving the bottle a gentle swirl, he watched as the dark vortex of elixir blended with the smooth color of the alcohol before the contents unified to a single shade of amber. He glared at the bottle and its contents then, hoping that his efforts wouldn't be in vain and that he might actually be able to numb the curse. He'd been holding in his rage—holding back what the magic inside of him demanded to shift him into every moment of every day—and the ongoing effort and the recent turn of events were taking a massive toll on him. Though it had barely been a full day since he'd last lost control—a loss of control that had nearly leveled an entire city block and sent one of the biggest therions he'd ever seen crying home with piss-stained pants—it was becoming obvious that it had only whetted its appetite for death and destruction rather than sating it.

And now he had the added stress of Gregori's wayward daughter and his power-abusing bastard of a son. The whole mess was enough to make him *want* to hand the reigns over to what writhed within him and take a little vacation in the back of his own mind; *anything* to rid him of the incessant burning in his skin and the burden of thought and responsibility! As the fumes of his rage made clear thoughts hazy, his tattoos continued to burn with their toxic inferno and driving him deeper into a place he knew he shouldn't go. Pulling his sleeves down in an effort to hide the cursed ink from both himself and the bar's patrons, he reflected more on the memories of the previous night.

To what lengths would the beast have gone if Zoey hadn't been there to stop him...?

Groaning, he took a long, hard pull from the bottle and shook his head.

"Fuck me sideways!" he muttered to himself, "What a mess!"

An undetermined length of time passed as he focused on *not* thinking about everything that was happening and putting as much of the supernaturally-spiked liquor into his system as possible. Finally, as he struggled to read the blurred label of a bottle behind the bar and wondering if the fat, old woman on the other side of the bar would be up for a quickie in the bathroom, he discovered that the bottle was empty and that he was officially and utterly wasted. Staring apprehensively at it, he was distantly aware of a lanky woman that was standing over him. He looked up at her, trying to focus past his foggy vision and an over-abundance of perfume. Between the sickeningly sweet floral stench, the dizzying effects of his cocktail, and his spinning head, he considered it a miracle that he wasn't already sick, but something in the woman's scent seemed to entice the beast and he realized that he might be able to bargain with it further if he gave it what it wanted.

"Care to join me outside?" she purred and leaned down, giving him a clear view of her assets through her V-neck and getting her painted lips dangerously close to his ear, to whisper "I know what you are, and I'm not afraid."

"Oh? You're not afraid, huh?" he scoffed and shook his head, noticing the bartender already glaring at him, "Then you obviously have *no* idea what I am!" He turned away from the old man and smirked. His body was alert and responding to the potential for both sex *and* blood, and he knew that his eyes had already begun to glow. As he grinned, he felt his canines extend and allowed them to show slightly through parted lips.

Cooing at the show, she stepped back and playfully covered her mouth in mock-surprise. "Oh my! You look parched! Perhaps I should give you a drink." She tapped her index finger against her throat and winked at him, "I know *exactly* what you're thirsty for, and I'll give you what you want."

"Ah! I get it! You're some kind of a pervert, right? You've got some kind of fucking feeder-fetish, or something?" he grumbled and looked away, disregarding his body's complaints over how long it had it been since he'd had *real* blood and not some synthetic crap that Zoey made in a lab. Though every fiber of his body was urging him to take her up on the offer, he remained seated; sneering at the idea of taking this bitch's charity just so she could get her rocks off. The whole notion was fucking disgusting, and the reality that some humans not only *knew* about them but actually *sought* them out posed a threat to their secrecy and opened the floodgates for the potential for careless second-generation sangs to inadvertently put countless numbers of freaks on the streets, and an army of mindless, insatiable.

Those ravenous third-generation vampires were nothing short of Hell on earth for *any* living thing in their path.

Like he didn't have enough problems already!

Zane growled and turned back to the woman to deny her the feed.

He was a split-second away from turning down the offer and telling off the woman when the beast surged forward and answered for itself. Having no control of his own actions, he rose from the stool and grabbed the woman's wrist and began to pull her outside. While he was neither subtle nor gentle, she didn't protest and nobody in the bar tried to stop him as he escorted her out the door.

He'd had enough with being nice, anyway!

"I love your tattoos," she purred when he'd finally gotten her to a secluded area in the parking lot, "I think vampires with ink are so sexy! You don't usually see too many, though, because of how fast your kind heal…" She caressed the exposed markings on his neck with her palms before moving to bring her lips to them.

"Don't do that!" he growled, slapping his hand over her mouth and pushing her away before she had a chance to kiss him. His vision cleared and the darkness receded as his eyes sparked with fury and narrowed at her. "If there is one rule that you should recognize it is this; do *not* touch them! *Ever!*"

She pouted and opened her mouth to protest his ruling. Not interested in anything she had to say, he returned his hand to her mouth to stop her voice. Feeling the warmth of her breath against his hand, he groaned and felt his fangs fully extend and winced slightly at the pain in his gums. Eyeing a prime spot on her shoulder, he moved in to pull her collar away; feeling a shiver travel through him as she let out a soft-yet-eager whimper and arched her neck to give him greater access. Moving his hand to her neck, he scratched her to open a gash so that he could drink. She gasped at the process, moaning and writhing as her blood began to seep to the surface and pushed towards him with growing anticipation. Not wanting to let her determine his pacing, he growled and pinned her to the wall to keep her from moving so he could coax his fangs back and calculate how he fed. If he allowed his saliva to enter her bloodstream, he'd risk turning her, and while the beast was giddy at the thought of creating a mindless killing machine *solely* to kill it, he fought the urge and pulled out the empty vial that he'd brought with him and moved to collect her blood inside it.

The woman whimpered as he went about the task and tried to push his hand away, "Wh-what are you doing? I want your mouth! Use your mouth! I *need* it!"

"Shut up! This is for your safety, idiot!" He held her down long enough to fill the vial and brought it to his lips to drink, finally getting the first drop of *real* blood onto his tongue.

Then he stopped.

He wretched and pulled away, tossing the vial and its contents to the ground and heaving. The blood! It was wrong! Oily and bitter and hot; *too* hot!

It wasn't human!

He snarled, spitting the lingering offense from his mouth again and again, as he narrowed his eyes at the woman; the *therion*!

The beast inside him, robbed of its chance to feed, shifted its focus from *drinking* her blood to *spilling* it. Growling, he grabbed her by the shoulders and shoved her against the wall with enough force to chip some of the bricks on the edge. She cried out, her eyes flashing momentarily with her true nature, as she gnashed her teeth at him and began to struggle against his grip.

"Let me go!" She shrieked, her voice shifting noticeably from her once sensual one to something far more bestial.

He hissed and tightened his hold, their struggle being spotlighted by his now-glowing tattoos. There was only one truth in his mind; one thing that he needed to focus on...therions were the enemy!

"Not fucking likely, bi—"

"Are you enjoying yourself, Zane?" a mocking voice interrupted from a short distance away.

Keith!

The unmistakable face of Gregori's son sneered at him; his greasy blonde-white hair slicked back and allowing the pretentious gaze of his blood-red irises to take the spotlight on his narrow, jagged face.

Both Zane and the beast within him agreed that their violent focus had a better and more deserving target. Still snarling, he spat at her. "Get lost, mutt," he growled, shoving her to the ground. The faint hiss of a silenced gunshot sounded a split-second before a bullet grazed his shoulder and he let out a loud growl as his body began to shake more. Turning his attention to the still-smirking Keith, he shook his head, glaring at the sleek pistol in his grip and felt his body's tremors double in intensity.

He wasn't going to be able to keep his rage contained.

Not this time.

Zane shook his head, trying to hold himself together, "Is this how somebody with a seat in The Council behaves when there are *innocents* around?"

"Innocents! *Innocents?* I see no innocence here! How 'bout you, girl? Is there any innocence in there?" Keith cackled and drove his gaze into the therion girl, "Come now, my pet! Show our friend what you are! Give him a glimpse of all that you truly can be!"

Zane frowned and looked over as the girl twitched and her eyes went glassy and empty before flashing brightly with the excitement of an awakened killer and her body began to shift and contort.

Zane frowned at the scene; something wasn't right. The way the therion's expression remained locked on him despite the violent transformation taking place was unnatural. Glancing back, he saw that Keith's gaze matched her own—his body rigid with focus and determination—and Zane realized that he'd taken control of her body; forcing her to do what he wanted with his aura! Though he couldn't see it in this form, he guessed that Keith's aura was extended and holding her mind from where he stood.

Taking several steps away from the woman as her body's spasms shifted her into a cat-like beast, Zane reached slowly in his coat to grab his Glock. Seeing the movement through the therion's eyes, the pair began to cackle as one before a clawed hand shot out at him and snatched away his gun, crushing the barrel and rendering it useless.

"Th-that"—Zane's face tightened and he felt a portion of his skull fracture over his left ear—"w-wa—Wwaaahhh!!—was our..." He snarled, pitching his head back-and-forth, and punched himself several times in his left temple, "*My!* That was *my* f-f-favorite gun!" He took a step towards Keith just as his right knee turned to dust and he was forced to kneel as a shriek of agony was drawn out. "GAH! FUCKING SHIT! Y-you... g-go-godDAM fucking shit-eatingGGAH!" His other knee gave out and his warping face crashed into the pavement and shattered his nose. A stream of howls and curses—choked and rendered indecipherable by the blood pooling in his throat—streamed forth right before a torrent of blood shot from his fresh bullet-wound as the muscles inflated all at once and rolled him to his side.

Keith and the therion watched, sharing the same calm expression of entertainment as they took in the show.

"D-don't—AHHH! FUCK! Fucking hell!—d-don't…" Zane whimpered and tried to feed his starving lungs but was throttled on a wave of pain as his spine reformed vertebrae-by-vertebrae. Though there was no air to fuel the words, his threats continued to flow: "… do-don't you *fucking* LAUGH at us!"

Keith chortled and looked around for effect, "Zane—my dear, psychotic friend—are you *lost*? Who, pray-tell, is 'us'?" He hauled back and drove the pointed toe of his dress shoes into Zane's chest, smirking as most of his ribs shattered audibly like the snapping of wet twigs. "Or are you *sharing* this broken bag of meat you call a body with another? Let's have a look-see at the damage…"

Zane's eyes flashed and shifted—a whirlwind of colors flooding his vision as the night went neon and shifted into a different spectrum—and he could suddenly see Keith's blood-red aura emerge from his chest like a hungry serpent and writhe towards him. The sight sparked something in Zane and beast, and both erupted into cackles that were funneled through their shared mouth and echoed into the night. Keith's aura wavered, pausing at the laughter and withdrawing slightly as Zane's dark-blue aura flickered like a dying flame before erupting into a fiery scarlet.

Both Keith and his mind-enslaved therion stepped back. "How in the hell—"

"We're just FULL of surprises, fucker!" Zane snarled, his aura firing forward and taking Keith by the throat. The symphony of shifting organs and reforming bones reached a crescendo then, and the beast—now fully emerged—stood and sneered. "It's time we made you pay!"

Keith gurgled and whimpered as he struggled to breathe through the auric hold the beast had on him. Unable to escape this now hulking creature that towered over both of them with disproportioned limbs that now surged with new muscle, their focus was lost upon seeing the leering, horrific face that was almost entirely occupied by a twisted, fang-filled grin and a pair of gold eyes that took them in with malice and hunger.

"We will *kill* you! We will make you *suffer*!" His voice rolled past blackened lips like magma as the auric tendril around Keith's neck playfully rolled at the base of his skull, "And in your dying moments, we will *RAPE* your every thought with torment until all there is left of your existence is *USSSSS*!"

With that, the beast invaded Keith's mind with its aura and ensnared his mind, crippling his hold on his motor functions and auric control.

Released from his hold, the therion's eyes widened as control was returned. As her awareness settled in, her gaze locked on the monster before her and she whimpered and fell back, scrambling to get away.

The beast growled, watching the therion flee the scene and disappear in the distance before smirking wickedly and shifting its gaze back to Keith.

"We can *SEE* inside your mind, *Keith*! And, soon enough,"— he traced a clawed finger across Keith's sternum in a slow slicing motion—"we will see inside the rest of you!"

Another bout of cackles issued.

"I…" Keith growled and narrowed his eyes, "… I got something to *show* you, then, you *abomination*!"

The beast's hold on Keith's mind tightened as all defenses dropped and a slideshow of memories began.

It was Gregori!

He was alive!

Alive?

How…?

The darkness surrounding Zane's mentor shifted and waned as Keith and the shadowed forms of several others emerged on the scene.

Echoes.

Fragmented words; shouting.

Gunshots.

Blood.

*"DO YOU SEE NOW, ZANE? ARE YOU DEEP
ENOUGH YET? HAVE YOU HAD YOUR FILL?"*

*The slideshow looped and reeled, reflecting Keith's memories of Gregori's
death—his* murder!*—in all corners of Zane's mind.*

*"YOU PAID TO SEE THE SHOW, ZANE! WOULDN'T
WANT TO HOLD ANYTHING BACK!"*

The beast's aura retracted, releasing its hold on Keith and
fleeing from the horrific visions. Head reeling, the ground came up
to meet it and Zane was distantly aware of the cold pavement and
his hot tears scorching down his twisted face. Though the tie had
been cut, Keith's visions burned and echoed inside him as he was
forced to relive that night with the new truth over and over and
over...

Keith had killed his own father!

Gregori's death was no accident!

"What's wrong?" Keith snarled, rubbing his throat as he spit
up a mouthful of blood on him and pulling out his gun once again,
"Too shook up to fight?"

"W-we are *NEVER* too shook up to fight, asshole!" Zane
roared, launching himself at Keith and swinging his massive arm in
a wide-arc at Keith's face.

The vampire growled and vanished before the attack could
land. Not about to let his enemy elude him, Zane jumped into
overdrive as well, his body and mind working exponentially faster
to allow for superhuman movement that was otherwise unseen by
the human eye. Keith's eyes reflected his rage as Zane met his pace,
rendering his gun useless as the two moved faster than any bullets
could.

Without knowing it, Keith had given him the advantage.

Though his curse was crippling to his mind, his body's ability
was nearly limitless! As blow-after-blow was landed, Keith's speed
began to waver; his energy rapidly dwindling.

And the beast was only getting started!

Overdrive was just another tool to kill, and the curse made

killing *very* simple. Control and reason were another story, however, and as his excitement and cockiness rose, his focus dwindled until…

Keith's aura shot out like a freight train that caught Zane square in the chest, throwing him out of overdrive, out of the alley, into the street, and embedding his body into the side of a parked car.

The car's alarm blared and pierced Zane's ears; filling his head with chaos. He struggled to block out the noise, crying out in agony as his senses were flooded. His massive body pitched and writhed in an effort to free itself from twisted metal as his warped tattoos began to glow brighter. Prying himself free, he stumbled forward and worked to steady his footing. The alarm's racket continued, and with every focus pulled towards the repetitive shrieks and flashing lights he lost sight of the rest of the world.

Again and again he brought his fists down on the car in an effort to silence it, but his actions only served to alter the pitch and tone and drive his rage further.

When he was certain that the alarm's howls would drag him over the edge, a red flash of light emerged and tore the battery from the hood—stopping the racket in an instant—and slammed it into the side of his head.

Dazed, he turned his attention to Keith as his aura retracted and he advanced casually towards him.

Zane let out a loud howl as he shot forward.

He needed to kill!

CHAPTER FOUR
CHAOS

"SERENA!" ZOEY'S EYES WENT WIDE as her body tensed, "We have to get to the city! Right now!"

"Whoa! What's the sudden rush?" Serena frowned, eyeing the auric skeptically, "Won't Zane have a shit-fit if we don't get back to the clan?"

"That's just it! It *is* Zane! He's... he's *trapped* in a... he's in a fight! He's in the city and... oh god! We have to hurry!" Zoey stammered.

Serena frowned, hearing the desperation and panic in Zoey's voice and nodded. "Hold on, this isn't going to be pleasant!" She warned, grabbing the auric by the wrist and rocketing down the street in overdrive. Though the added weight made her movement sloppy and lagging, they were still able to make the journey in only a few seconds. Seeing they were close, Serena shifted back to a normal speed and stared in shock at the chaos as Zoey struggled to come to grips with the sudden change in scenery.

The sound of alarms and the stench of smoke filled the night, and the air was so saturated in auric energy that Serena could actually hear it hum. She frowned, seeing that Zoey was still dazed from the trip and barely able to stand, and tried to get a lock on Zane's auric signature.

Who in the hell was he fighting anyway?

She stepped to the smoke-filled streets, blinded by the thick haze and forced to follow her other senses.

"You're going to have to do better than that!"

Serena frowned, a violent surge filling her at the familiarity of the voice in the distance and she charged towards it. In an instant the air went clear—the smoke being held back by an immense auric force—and she found herself face-to-chest with a...

"WHAT IN THE FUCK?" she cried out and tried to back-peddle, stumbling and falling back. The monster's ears perked and its eyes closed in like Hellish spotlights on her. "Wh-who... *what* are you?" she stammered as the beast stepped closer and loomed over her and threw a fist the size of a beer keg at her. "Oh go—Zane! Help!"

The monster's attack froze only inches from her and she whimpered, blinking against a pocket of air that carried specks of dust and ash into her eyes. Startled, she looked up into the gold eyes of her would-be attacker; its face shifting from one of fury and murderous rage to something soft and nervous.

Biting her lip, she started to stand, hoping her movement wouldn't spark the monster's anger again.

But it only stared, blinking and whimpering.

"S-Ser-en-a…"

Her eyes widened, "Za—"

"Well, isn't this just precious? The beast has a soft spot for you, sis," the painfully familiar and condescending voice chimed in behind her.

She growled and spun to face her brother, "Keith!" A new surge of anger welled within her as her brother's smirking face came into view and she instinctively formed her auric bow in her hand, "What the hell are you doing here?"

"Missed you too, you horrid little bitch, I'm sure we have so much to catch up on. However, in case you haven't noticed, I *am* rather busy and now is not the time to reminisce. I have a bit of unfinished business to conduct with our late-father's favorite project."

Serena! Watch out! Devon's voice echoed in her head just as Keith threw his aura at them. The world shook and the street cratered as the blast connected and Serena felt the ground vanish beneath her as the Zane-monster scooped her up and pulled her against his massive body and shielding her against the flames and debris as they singed and punctured his back. Sensing the pained surge in Zane's now-red aura, Serena's eyes widened and she disbanded her auric bow to try and shield him against further harm. The damage had already been done, however, and he let out an agonized howl as his knees buckled and a pool of blood grew at their feet.

"Oh god, Zane! What's—"

"Don't!" His voice made her flinch, "We're…" He growled and shook his head, "I'm fine!"

She glanced up, about to call him on his obvious lie but was only able to cry out as he lifted her and jumped out of the range of another of Keith's attacks and landed on the rooftop of a used car dealership. Though he'd gotten them clear of the danger, his injuries proved too severe and he buckled and collapsed shortly after setting her down. He groaned, writhing and heaving, as his hulking body seized and his aura inflated and grew bright enough to force her to shield her eyes.

A pained cry issued out that made her insides shift and she tried to squint past the glare of his aura to see what was happening to him. After a moment, the blood-colored orb dimmed and collapsed, turning back to Zane's familiar blue as it lazily bobbed around his broken and naked body; his mismatched eyes swimming in his skull before focusing on her.

"Serena...?"

"Jesus... Zane! What... what's happen—" The gentle sound of steps approaching cut off Serena's panic and she turned, her aura flaring as she hissed at her brother, "Keith! I don't know what this is about, but I swear on our mothe—"

"Oh shut up, you self-righteous cunt!" His aura spiked and he bared his fangs, "You couldn't hold your own in a challenge against me when you were in your prime! And you and I can *both* see those days have long-since left you a husk of our family's former glory! Now step aside before I'm forced to make an example out of yo— AHHH!" Keith dropped to one knee as the jagged remains of a parking meter—now a makeshift spear that flooded the rooftop in blood-covered coins—jutted through his shoulder.

"I think you should go, Keith," Zoey floated gracefully to the rooftop with another three parking meters orbiting her in an auric grip, "before *I'm* forced to create a job-opening in The Council!"

"Gah!" Keith gripped the hunk of metal protruding from him and winced in pain, his aura whipping and darting chaotically, "You wretch! You sodding—Ah! Dammit!—interfering little whelp! I'll see to it that you're all made examples of!" Focusing his aura, Keith gripped the meter with his aura and yanked it free, crying out as he did. As his breathing steadied, he narrowed his eyes at Serena, "I don't know what you *think* is going to happen, but you'll see in time the error of becoming involved with these peons!"

"God dammit, Keith! What is this all about?" Serena demanded, drawing back her auric bow.

Standing, he shook his head, "In due time, Serena. When I'm not..." He glanced at his bleeding shoulder, "Well... when I'm better equipped to handle my affairs, I'll see about showing you some degree of mercy."

Serena drew back her aura, preparing to strike, "Don't do me any favors, you little shit!"

Keith smirked and shrugged, stepping away from the three and towards the rooftop's edge, "Consider it sibling hospitality, then, but I assure you that you'll not want what's coming to them."

And then he was gone; vanishing into overdrive.

"God damn you, Keith!" Serena snarled, releasing her aura and running to where he'd been standing in the hopes of seeing some sign of him in the distance, "Don't you dare run off! You fucker! Get you and your cryptic bullshit get back here NOW!" She screamed out.

"Serena, stop! He's gone!" Zoey was still shaking from earlier. She turned to Zane's unconscious body and shook her head, "We need to get him to the clinic! Fast!"

"But what about—" Serena frowned as the first wail of sirens sounded in the distance. She knew that the cops, fire department, EMT, and anybody else with any authority in the humans' world would be crawling all over the place soon enough, and it was in their better interests to not be standing around —beaten, bloody, and accompanying an unconscious, naked man—when they arrived. She growled and nodded, abandoning her hopes of tailing Keith, "Let's go."

"Thank God for small favors!" Serena grumbled as she used her aura to steal the keys to one of the cars on the dealership's lot, "I don't know what we'd do if I had to try and hotwire a ride."

"I still don't see why we have to *steal* the car!" Zoey frowned, hoisting Zane into the back seat of the convertible with her aura.

Serena sighed, "Because I left my checkbook at home! God, Zoey, are you *serious*? If we're standing around when the flashing lights show up do you think us *jacking a car* when there's all *this*"—

she motioned to all the damage in the streets and finished her arc with a nod to Zane—"is *really* going to be their main focus? We'll be lucky if we aren't brought in as *terrorists*! Besides, he's too heavy for us to carry and I can't travel with *both* of you in overdrive!"

Zoey blushed. "I suppose that's true…"

"Fuckin' A it's true! Now get in!" Serena hopped over the driver-side door and nestled into the cushioned leather seat and ran her fingers over the steering wheel with her left hand as she fed the stolen key into the ignition. "Oh, baby! Where you been all my life?"

Zoey frowned and looked over. "What was that?"

Serena pouted and shrugged, "I said 'this'll have to do'."

Zoey frowned and shook her head, sighing nervously. "Should we at least leave a note or something?" she asked, chewing her lip.

"Nah. The thing's probably insured, and if it's not they have it coming. Besides, what would you write? 'So sorry to have stolen your car. Better luck next time'? Yea, real badass!" She shook her head and shifted into gear before slamming the accelerator to the floor and rocketing out of the lot, "Where's your sense of adventure?"

Zoey whimpered, pressing her hands against the dashboard to secure herself, "I… I think I left it back there, actually!"

Serena rolled her eyes and turned sharply onto the next street, running the light and hopping the curb as she did. "Shit! The steering's loose! Piece of junk!" She frowned as the sirens' wails grew louder and she realized they were coming from ahead. "Aw, dammit! Zoey, a little help?"

"If I do will you slow down?"

"Not likely, but at least we won't have an entourage of law-enforcement following us all the way back to the clan!"

Zoey groaned in defeat.

Serena smiled, "Knew I could count on you!"

As the emergency response crew neared, both Serena and Zoey's auras darted out, entering each and every mind and cloaking their escape as they passed.

"God damn, Zoey! We make one hell of a—" the headlights of an ambulance caught the windshield as it changed lanes, the driver unaware of the car in its path due to the pair's auric blinders, and Serena flinched as the impending collision approached. In an instant, the world around them went blue as Zoey's aura wrapped around the car and yanked it to the left and out of the path of destruction. "Holy shit!" Serena's eyes went wide as she watched the tail lights of the ambulance disappear in the rearview mirror, "I mean, wow; *that* was adventurous, huh? Look at that, they took off the mirror on your side!" She cackled and slapped her left knee, "Damn, Zoey! I should drive with you more often!"

"I think I'm going to be sick!" Zoey cried out, still bracing herself.

"Oh c'mon, ya big baby! We did it!" Serena laughed wildly as she ran another light to make a hair-pin turn.

"Oh god! We're going to die!" Zoey squeaked.

"Is he going to be okay?" Zoey's already soft voice was nervous and shaken.

Zane groaned and struggled to open his eyes, but found his lids heavy and unresponsive. He sighed and, still rolling on what he assumed was a sedative-induced calm, enjoyed the serenity while it lasted. Though he couldn't see, he recognized the energies of the clan and found further comfort in knowing that they'd made it back safely.

And that was about all that made sense to him at that moment.

He recalled the fight—the familiar rage and the overpowering impulse to murder and destroy—and he *also* remembered seeing Serena.

And then he remembered...

Clarity?

Peace?

That couldn't have been right. Nothing about the curse was

clear, and there certainly was nothing *peaceful* about it; nothing! Perhaps Serena or Zoey had altered his memories to cover up some horrible act…?

He was just beginning to test his mental condition to see if something hinted towards auric tampering when a second voice interrupted his thoughts; "It looks like he won't have any prolonged injuries. His wounds were pretty severe, but his… er, unique condition seems to have repaired a lot of the damage. He's also responding positively to the enchanted synth-blood we have him on, but we're still monitoring for any lingering damage to his psyche. We should know for certain in a day or two when the swelling in his head's gone down."

"That's a relief," Zoey said with a heavy exhale, "The big dummy! This was the *second* time he'd transformed in less than 24 hours! Every time it happens I can sense his pain from all the way across town! I don't know how many times he can go through that before his body…" Zoey's voice trailed off.

Zane tried to move again—to will some response that would tell Zoey he was awake—but his body was still unresponsive.

"It's hard to tell. He's not *built* for the process. While I don't understand exactly *what* it is that does this, it certainly hasn't helped him to endure the physical strain. Every time he changes—both *into* and *out of* that… thing—his body *and* his mind are literally broken. He isn't so much being transformed as something is rebuilding him, but any biological response that could numb or moderate the pain seems to be held back, and if our scans are accurate, then it would appear the same response is actually *keeping* his system from going into shock. Not only is the pain *not* being suppressed, his body's actually *working* to stay conscious so he's forced to endure it! It's as though whatever it is those tattoos do *wanted* him—"

"Listen," Serena's voice cut into the med-tech's explanation, "this is fascinating and all—not to mention *incredibly* reassuring to hear—but maybe now isn't the best time. What I'm hearing and what this all boils down to is 'he's suffered, he's suffering, and he's doomed to suffer yet again' and while I'm sure this is making Zoey feel so much better—'cuz, hell, your bedside manner is spot-fucking-on!—I'd say all your reassurance has put us both in such a positive frame of mind that we may just burst into song. Problem is, I'm tone-deaf and I have—get this!—actually *killed* housecats with my voice. So, while I'm eager to have more of your sunshine blown up our asses, I'd *hate* to cause an untimely death on your staff with my lyrical exuberance. So how 'bout you give us a moment alone with our friend, huh?"

Had it not been for Zane's inability to speak and move he was certain he'd have fallen out of bed with laughter, and he once again cursed his unresponsive muscles at the realization that he couldn't applaud the Vailean girl's superb delivery. The silence—save for the rapid clacking of the med-tech's retreating footsteps—was both a blessing and a curse. Though he hated the prolonged silence, the explanation had been—though nothing new to him—depressing and unsettling. Thankfully, Serena's brashness had been more than enough to end it.

Did she know he was awake?

Had she done it for his sake?

Though she had opted not to hear of his curse from their clan's staff, he was certain that she was far from being over her curiosity. He would, no doubt, still have to explain everything to her sooner or later. If nothing else he owed her that much.

Hearing her voice *had* calmed him though, and the more he thought about it the more he was forced to admit that he wasn't imagining that fact. No matter how he approached the situation, there was no denying that the monster's destructive nature had been squelched upon her arrival; had allowed his reason and focus to return so he could keep them both alive.

But *why?*

Why would the beast's fury—a fury that had proven on *many* occasions to dwindle only *after* everything and everyone around it had been destroyed—yield to *anybody.*

And why her?

Could her ties to Gregori truly be *that* influential on something that was nothing less than rage and chaos incarnate?

Surely it couldn't be her gender; the beast didn't care for anyone. Male or female.

And none of the women on his mile-long list of past flings had ever swayed or stayed the perpetual mayhem in his mind.

Hell! The only impact they'd had on it was encouraging him to make it hurt.

But all the hair-pulling and rough fuck sessions had only ever been just that.

Nothing but a one night stand.

So why her?

Why now?

He heard more footsteps start up and fade into the distance, followed shortly after by the sound of the door as it was pushed open and then slowly closed with a sigh, and he wondered if he had been left alone with nothing more than his drug-hazed thoughts. He tried again to pry open his eyes, putting all his conscious effort into getting *some* control—no matter how small; *anything* to feel like his body was his own—and succeeded in getting them to gradually flutter open and was rewarded with a bright white light that bled past his parted lids. As the beams of fluorescence assaulted his wide pupils he hissed and tried to turn his face away.

"Jeez!" Serena jumped a short ways away as his noise and movement cut through the still silence, "God! You big dummy! Scared me to Hell-and-back! Oh, and for the record, you should've left your eyes closed," Serena's condescending tone was laced with one of concern that gave her away as she leaned over him to adjust the light away—hanging on a swinging fixture over his bed—out of his line of sight.

He looked around for a moment, relishing in his returning motor functions, and allowed his gaze to finally come to rest on Serena.

He bit his lip.

She was so close to him.

Too close to him!

He caught a whiff of her subtle scent—sweet and floral with something spicy mingled throughout, and visions of cherry blossoms and cinnamon sticks surfaced in his mind—and, getting lost in the enticing aroma, allowed himself to inhale it further again and again. It was too compelling to experience only once; demanding to be recognized and worshipped repeatedly. It was the smell of nature and beauty. Her long hair—the color of sunlight reflected on fresh snow—was tied back into a tight ponytail, and while he found the vision an enticing one, he couldn't help but feel a tugging desire to pull it free of its confines. He frowned as he caught his left hand shifting and beginning to rise towards her and forced himself to pull away, shaking his head softly at himself.

He would never allow himself to fall in love; *could* never allow himself to fall in love.

Not with anyone!

Not with this curse!

Destroying everything and everyone was what it thrived upon, and any feelings he had for anybody would make it all the more painful when he tore their still-beating hearts from their fractured ribcages.

"Why didn't you tell me the truth?" she asked softly.

He sighed, keeping his gaze locked to the sterile-white ceiling tiles, "I wasn't sure if you were ready to hear it."

"Did Keith do it? Was he the one who killed my father?" her voice was shaking, but he couldn't tell if it was from grief or rage.

"He…" He growled and closed his eyes again, not wanting to risk seeing her expression upon hearing the truth, "He was. It seems he's assigned himself with a mission to take this clan apart from the inside. It's all part of some fucking vendetta against your father, and he *knew*!"—he felt his hands tighten into sharp fists—"Your father saw it coming and I…" Zane forced himself to settle down. Obviously the drugs were beginning to wear off. "It doesn't matter. All you need to know is that it *was* Keith's doing."

Serena pursed her lips and looked away, trying—but failing—

to conceal the shimmering wetness in her eyes. After several deep breaths, she opened her mouth and stretched her jaw before deciding she was in control of her emotions.

Zane knew that look all too well.

She sighed, "My brother and I never got along; to be honest with you, and I don't think *anybody* got along with the bastard. He was always up to something—always plotting some terrible new prank or some sadistic new way to torture… well, anybody!—and using our father's role as leader as a means of getting away with it all." She shook her head, her face starting to melt into a mask of rage, "He *always* used power and influence as an excuse to do *anything* he wanted. He's never *not* been a manipulative, fucking dick, and I never did anything to stop it. I was too fucking scared of him!"

Zane frowned and looked at her, "Serena?"

She was still shaking her head; still staring off with growing fury, "I think this fight has always been mine. He hated that Daddy saw me as his princess—as the only one fit to take over the Clan of Vail—and now he's using the fear I had of him when we were children to try and scare me away from this. All so he can prove that our father's judgment was wrong. I just was too selfish to fight back…" She confessed, "… until now."

Zane's eyes widened and he stared, dumbfounded and awed, "Then… you're *accepting* the clan? You'll help us?"

"Bitch, please! I am *done* being under that arrogant turd's boot. Besides, you wouldn't make it that far without me, anyway!" She gave him a coy smirk before shaking her head, "I can't help but wonder how he's gotten control of The Council's approval for all of this, though…"

"He hasn't. Well, not completely, at least. Not *yet*. He still needs…" Zane sighed, shaking his head as he paused. Realizing for the first time that they were the only two in the room and what that meant. He frowned, "Where's Zoey?"

CHAPTER FIVE
DOWNFALL

ZOEY WAS EXHAUSTED.

The end result of the previous night's chaos had all-but driven her six feet under, and seeing Zane laid out on in the infirmary was just too much for her. While she wanted nothing more than to drop into her bed and allow sleep to consume her, she was unable to get settled enough to sleep. For nearly four hours she tossed and turned—her fleeting moments of sleep haunted by visions of the strange therion from the forest—and, upon each awakening, she was forced to admit more and more the impact he had had on her.

When it was finally dark enough for her to sneak out without notice, she quickly took advantage of the situation and snuck out; using her aura to scan for potential witnesses and seeing to it that they would recall witnessing *nothing*. Though there was a twinge of guilt at using her abilities against her own clan-mates—and for such selfish and, moreover, childish pursuits—she couldn't shake her hopes to finally have some time to herself in the forest.

Though she was secretly hoping that she wouldn't be alone.

Sighing and allowing her mind to wander, she let her surroundings become a distant thought until she was finally in the depths of the forest. Not knowing how to seek out the source of her restlessness, she momentarily abandoned her hopes and went to her regular spot in the center of a clearing where the canopy of trees opened up just enough to allow her to see the moon. Settling in the rim of this clearing, she leaned against one of the thicker tree trunks that served as the dividing line and closed her eyes as her thoughts shifted once again to the therion from the previous night. She bit her lip and lifted her hand to her chest; she *knew* it was wrong to obsess over somebody that was, for all intents and purposes, the enemy, but she was unable to think about the therion as anything evil or malicious. Again and again she pushed the thoughts below the surface of her bubbling mind, yet, each time, they would burst back to the surface—that much stronger and more compelling—and she felt her heartbeat quicken and lodge itself in her throat.

What was going on with her?

Closing her eyes, she began to hum softly as she accepted the inevitability of her own mind's desires and allowed her thoughts to caress the forbidden territory.

"You again?" the familiar voice snarled from overhead and Zoey's eyes flew open and shifted upward towards the dark mask of night-bathed leaves, "What are you doing here? I thought I told you to stay away!" His voice echoed down, though she could not see where he was.

"I-I'm sorry!"—she lied—"I was just trying to relax."—

another lie—"I didn't mean to! I swear! I didn't even think you'd *be* here again!" Zoey bit her lip, mentally counting how many lies she'd just fed him and wondering how many he'd believe. Still looking up in the direction of the voice, she moved to pull away from the tree.

Though she couldn't convince herself he was an enemy, she couldn't be sure that he shared her sentiments and worried that he was going to attack.

A growl echoed from the canopy and Zoey froze as the sound of branches shifting picked up and the object of her desires dropped down gracefully to his feet, "Don't worry, I'm not interested in killing you. I don't need any more issues than I already have," he sighed, shifting his eyes to the ground.

"Really?" she felt herself smile and her face went red from the reaction. She could see from the calmness in his earthy aura that he was being honest, and this realization motivated her to take a step towards him. Realizing what she was doing, she paused and looked into his mind, positive that he'd be furious if he knew of the invasion but unable to refrain from finding out more about him. Though the depths of his mind were clouded and hazy—feeling like a dense fog and containing more images and memories than calculated thoughts—she "saw" that he was wondering her name but was unsure of how to ask. Smiling uncontrollably again, she withdrew her prying aura and took another step, "I'm Zoey."

"Zoey…" He recited the name under his breath, sounding confused and looked over at the small lake nearby that was shimmered under the moonlight and reflected the flashes from the dancing fireflies before shifting his predatory gaze back to her and nodding once. "You can call me 'Isaac'."

He sighed and played with the idea of running off, knowing that he should leave before this became something more severe than what it already was. It wasn't right to get close to a vampire,

no matter what. Not after his experience with their kind. He knew
he was supposed to kill vampires on sight. After all, it was his job
to do so...

... no matter how much he hated it.

"Isaac? I like that name," she smiled and gestured for him to
sit with her near the tree he'd been perching in, "Do you want to
sit with me?"

He turned towards her and frowned, she looked fragile—*too*
fragile, like the slightest contact would break her—as she held out
her tiny arm. He inhaled slowly, looking back towards the direction
of his pack and weighing his options for a moment before looking
back at her and letting his eyes trace her body.

Though she was a vampire, there was no denying that she *was*
beautiful. The intense blue of her shimmering eyes and dyed hair
adorning a soft and innocent face reminded him of a sunny day and
he felt a warm flush overcome him as this thought came.

Just like the previous night, he found himself reaching for her
and quickly pulled away and looked down, feeling the warmth
replaced by a flood of embarrassment. Her gaze was completely on
him, taking in everything they saw—and more, he suspected—and
her piercing eyes filled him with a sense of comfort and stability he
had never felt before. He averted his eyes again, afraid that the
calmness would make him weak and vulnerable to an attack. Could
she be creating a distraction; setting him up while another leech
attacked from the darkness? But he couldn't convince himself that
the suspicions were justified. Something in the way she looked at
him made him feel...

Something he shouldn't.

"So, what were you doing out here before you found me?" she
smiled and sat back against the neighboring tree and looked out at
the pond.

"I was trying to clear my mind," he answered before frowning.
He wasn't usually this open—this honest—with anybody.

"Oh? I was too," she smiled again, "I always come here when I
need to think. It's so relaxing here!" Her smile widened; her voice

was soft and filled with so much passion and excitement, "I've always loved it here!"

He blushed and, without moving his head, shifted his eyes towards her, finding himself getting lost in everything about this enticing, albeit unusual, vampire.

He forced himself to look away again.

To become involved with their kind was the *last* thing he wanted. He had a mission to follow—a job that he'd dedicated himself to seeing through—and he couldn't help but feel guilty for the thoughts and feelings in his mind.

He didn't need to see her to know she was smiling. Something about her had a sincerity behind it, and he couldn't help but feel that it *was* real; that it wasn't just a setup. Though he barely knew her, he felt like he could talk to her about anything. He growled and shook his head.

This was not supposed to happen!

It couldn't happen!

"Is something wrong?" she frowned at the noise.

"No. It's nothing. I was just thi—" He paused and looked over his shoulder, hearing footsteps drawing near. He inhaled, drawing in the scent of the forest through his nostrils to identify the owner of the steps and groaned as he realized who was approaching. "You need to hide. Now!

She frowned and followed his gaze and bit her lip as she realized what was happening, "But what about—"

"Do as I said if you want to stay alive! Hide and don't come out until I say so! Do whatever you can to mask your scent and don't make a noise!" He stood and stepped towards her in one fluid motion, grabbing her and easily lifting her to her feet before pushing her out of the clearing. The brief contact of their touch sparked something within him and he frowned at the sensation, quickly turning away, and waiting for the company to cross into the clearing.

Zoey stayed quiet as she wrapped her aura around herself to keep the newcomer from sensing her.

"There you are," a husky female voice chimed from behind the bushes as she and another female therion approached him, "We were wondering where you'd wandered off to."

"Shouldn't you be back with the others and preparing?" Isaac's posture went from relaxed to ramrod-straight as soon as the two emerged.

"Aw, but without you it's no fun!" She stuck out a far-too-large bottom lip in a seductive mockery of a pout, "Besides, more of his kin have arrived and they are cruel! Far crueler than the last!"

"I know that. But, there's nothing else I can do about this Keith or his followers right now."

She frowned at this, "But you're our *leader*! We can't just—"

"That's right! And *as* the leader I have to make a choice that might get a lot of you killed. Until we know how it will affect us, we do nothing more than what we've been doing! Do you understand?"

The two whimpered and nodded.

He shook his head, clearly irritated, and threw out his hand to point off in the distance; directing them to leave. "Go. Both of you! We can't afford a conflict with them; not now. I'll be back soon."

"But we're tired of them!" The one began to step forward, obviously not liking his answer, "It's been three cycles already and you *still* haven't chosen a ma—"

He growled and narrowed his eyes at her, "I'm not dealing with this now!"

The other therion tugged at the first's shoulder, "Come on. He's never taken a female before. Why would he change that now?" she glared at him, driving the accusation further.

The other girl nodded slowly and turned to her friend, whimpering softly.

"Do not test my patience any further than you have! I've dealt with enough already without having you and the others cause any more problems! Now get back to the others! Don't make me say it again." He flashed them his teeth, his eyes glowing bright in the moonlight and they scampered off.

Once they were completely out of sight and earshot, Isaac called out: "You can come out now, vampire!" Though his posture and tone had shifted from a moment earlier, he didn't turn away from where the two female therions had been standing.

"You know you can call me Zoey!" She pouted as she stepped out.

"What's wrong with 'vampire'? It's what you are, isn't it? Why would you think it a bad title?" he asked curiously, cocking his head to one side.

"I guess because even though it's *what* I am, it's not *who* I am."

Isaac frowned, not sure of how to take her statement and watched as she brushed her knees. He frowned at the realization that his curiosity had returned, and he suddenly wanted to learn more about her and her mind. He let out a heavy breath and leaned against a tree, "Should you *really* be spending time with your enemy?"

She smirked and shrugged. "I could ask you the same thing," she stuck out her tongue before plopping down next to him, "And plus"—she blushed and looked down—"I think you're interesting. Besides, I'm allowed to talk to whomever I want! Especially since our clan is in between leaders." She frowned at her own confession, knowing that Gregori wouldn't have liked her talking to a therion either, let alone revealing clan secrets.

He grinned and turned his attention to her and arched his eyebrow, "You find me *that* interesting, eh?"

She paused and blushed, delighted that he'd overlooked the politics of the situation but embarrassed nonetheless, and began to stammer before realizing nothing coherent was emerging and shut her mouth abruptly. He laughed and shook his head, watching the moon in the pond and sighed.

"You're not half bad yourself. In fact, I'd go so far to say you are interesting as well. I mean, for a vampire and all, I guess," he shot her a coy smirk.

She faked a pout and punched Isaac softly in the arm before giggling, "Well, thank you… I guess."

Before she could pull her hand back he grabbed her wrist and held it in his large hand and frowned, confused at his own actions. She blushed at the contact but didn't flinch or try to pull free, but instead shifted her hand to meet his grip. His gaze descended to the foreign sight of their clasped hands and he watched as she squeezed his fingers and returned his gaze with her brightly lit blue eyes; eyes that both challenged him and made him feel whole.

She was beautiful inside and out.

He couldn't help but smile despite the single truth that burned in his mind; she was going to be his downfall.

Though weakness and defeat had long-since been something for him to avoid at all costs, he couldn't bring himself to pull away despite this fact.

And *that* made him more afraid than he ever could have imagined.

He was *supposed* to hate vampires—all vampires!—and yet here he sat, feeling driven to do the unspeakable with this gorgeous female.

Instead, in clear defiance of himself and his kind, he acknowledged his need to taste her.

Her lips called to his and he suddenly needed to feel them against his. His heart had felt so cold, driving him away from the numerous advances of countless females of his pack again and again, but suddenly he felt a spark and wanted nothing more than to take this new warmth into him and make it his.

Being with this vampire made his blood boil again.

She had closed her eyes as he leaned closer and he could feel an exhale of anticipation from her as he dipped his head in and pressed his lips to hers.

Zoey gasped as the therion pressed his lips to hers!

Was this real?

Her mind was reeling; spinning and dragging her more and more into him. All logic—all the past truths and orders and teachings—was burned away by the fire spreading within her. With all she had once held on to gone, the only certainty in her mind was that she never wanted to leave this place.

She lifted her arms and wrapped them carefully around his neck to pull him in tighter. He matched her efforts as she felt his strong hands at her waist as he pulled her against his body.

Zoey gave him complete control, not caring what he did to her at that point, and moaned at the intensity of it all. She felt herself get lost in him—aching and driving to entangle herself all the more within his essence—and refused to worry about where it might take her. Never before had she felt this way; so powerful and yet so helpless and, through the chaos, so goddam beautiful. She knew he was her enemy and yet, she couldn't find any reason to let go.

Slowly, they drew away from one-another, both breathing heavily and letting their lids open to reveal the others' gaze. Neither wanting to release the hold on the other and they just stared at the other for a moment longer.

Zoey knew then that he was going to be her downfall; that he had her so entirely under the power of his passion that there was nothing she wouldn't do to find herself back in its depths.

And, while she couldn't bring herself to care about what happened to her, she had no way of pushing away the burning truth and under no circumstances could she risk her comrades; no matter the situation, she couldn't bring herself to threaten the Clan of Vail.

And this—Isaac and his people—were too much of a threat to

Vail's security...

She felt her breath lock in her chest, knowing that she couldn't allow her heart's desires to go any further. In their vulnerable state and without a leader there was no solid defense against an attack.

She couldn't do that to them...

"I... I need to go. I've been gone... and the others will worry if I don't get home soon. I'm sorry, Isaac," she bit her lip, fighting the welling tears as she took in his face once more, and turned away before he had a chance to respond. As more and more distance was put between them, she felt his aura begin to shrivel and stutter with his growing sadness, and as she stepped out of range and lost the heart-wrenching ache from his mind—leaving her only with her own—she heard a pained howl echo through the forest.

CHAPTER SIX
PASSION

"SO WHAT SHOULD OUR NEXT STEP be? If we wait too long we may find ourselves too late to stop what's coming," Zane growled as he sat at the desk with Serena and Zoey. Zoey was quieter than usual—seeming preoccupied and distant to the business at hand—and he turned to her, pausing for a moment to wait for her attention to shift. When her vacant stare remained, he shook his head and moved on. Without being certain that something was wrong he wasn't about to bombard her with questions.

Not yet anyway.

"We need to make a plan of action. Those damned dogs will be coming soon, I'm sure," he shook his head, "Keith's an impatient prick, and his hold over the mutts will only last so long before they turn on him too."

Zoey's eyes shifted at the mention of the therions and she sighed, nodding, "Well, before we can do *anything*, Serena needs to be trained."

"Hey! I can fight!" Serena glared and ignored Devon as he chuckled inside her mind.

Zoey blushed and nodded, "It's not that you're not strong—nothing could be farther from the truth—but your methods *are*, while impressive, unconventional. It'd be better to put them to the test in the safety of a training course rather than in the middle of a battle when it can mean somebody's life."

Zane turned to Serena and offered a gentle smile and she felt Devon's anger flare up from his gaze. He clearly didn't like the way Zane watched her. He was still fuming over his inability to protect her the other night from Keith and being forced to watch as the vampire-beast saved her instead.

Serena had been right; she would need to find a body for him sooner than he thought. He wouldn't be able to stand being nothing more than a shadow much longer.

He watched Zane more carefully and grinned. Serena *did* seem drawn to him, and there was no denying that she'd liked it the one night when he'd taken control of him. Thinking of that night—the way Serena had felt under his stolen touch and her response to something other than his voice—he became more and more certain of what had to be done. While he was thankful for Serena's loyalty to him, he knew it would only last so long before the need for something more drove her into the arms of another.

And *that* was something he would not allow!

"Zoey *is* right, Serena. Though you're clearly very skilled, your combat approach is too chaotic. Somebody with Keith's level of control and training would find an opening in your attacks too quickly. You'll need to train more," Zane nodded, standing and motioning for her to follow, "Let's go."

Still scowling over their words, Serena stood and stepped through the doors with him.

Catching up to Zane, they walked side-by-side in complete silence as she was led through the levels of the clan's headquarters and, finally, into a large training room that occupied most of the building's basement. Serena looked around at the immense room, taking in the white padded walls and racks adorned with weapons that seemed to stretch on endlessly. The array of blades and bludgeons, staffs and spears, and just about any fashion of axe she could hope to raise over her head for a killing blow brought a grin to her previously sunken face. The collection was a thing of dreams!

Well... *her* dreams, at least.

"I am *SO* not going easy on you!" She smirked and followed after him further inside the training room, "First moment I get, I'm taking off a finger!"

Zane raised an eyebrow and turned his entire body to face her, "You sure you're ready to spar against me? You may have got me the other night, but to be fair, it was never my intention to bring you in damaged. Now—with a med-staff handy and enough synthetic blood to heal anything not fatal—I have no reason to be gentle."

"That's fine with me," she turned away and scoffed, "I *like* it rough! Besides, how tough can you be? You *were* just injured and laid-out."

He shrugged out of his shirt and smirked, his fangs already extended in excitement, "Don't worry about that, little lady. I heal fast."

Serena took in the view, finally getting a good look at his tattoos in all their glory. Under the evenly-spaced and all-revealing lighting of the training center she could make out every intricate trace of the tribal patterns that covered most of his torso. A memory of her lips tracing the designs from the night Devon had possessed him surfaced and she bit her lip, suppressing it as fast as it came.

"Stay focused! A distracted mind is a mind that's eager to be destroyed! And I can already see that you are elsewhere! If your father taught me anything, it's that you can't let your emotions run rampant in the battlefield," Zane scolded as he grabbed two sparring sticks and tossed one in her direction.

Serena glared and grabbed the staff in midair with her aura and drew it to her hand slowly as she dropped into a fighting stance. Keeping the blunt tip of her weapon aimed at her opponent, she grinned at him, "What's the matter? You afraid to give me something sharp?"

"We wouldn't want Daddy's little girl to hurt herself on her first day of classes!" Zane smirked and immediately charged her straight-on, holding his staff at one end and letting its length trail after him as he rocketed towards her. As the distance between them rapidly dwindled, he pivoted and went to swing at her; bringing the entire length around in a wide, hissing arc with all the momentum he had gathered.

Seeing his direct approach, Serena smirked and vanished. As the end of the staff broke through the air where she'd been standing a moment ago, he growled.

Of course the girl knew how to go into overdrive!

And that meant she would try to…

He brought the staff around and held it behind him—letting the length run parallel with his spine—in time to deflect Serena's attempt to attack him from behind. The thunderous impact of the two weapons coming together filled the room and was quickly absorbed into the padding as Zane spun to face her.

But she was already gone again!

He smiled at her tenacity as he pushed himself into overdrive. As his vision shifted to accommodate the new speed, he spotted her as she sprinted in a semi-circle to try and take him from the side. Spinning around to deflect her attack, he came in with the opposite end in an attempt to catch her behind her leading ankle, only to have her move that foot in time to avoid the strike...

... and drive it into his stomach.

The force from the kick was enough to knock him back, but Zane was able to stay both on his feet and in overdrive as she came at him again. As the vicious attacks continued, both held strong against the other, the combined force of their strikes straining the staffs and filling the room with a prolonged roar of supernatural battle. Another strike was thrown and blocked and both of the weapons gave out under the other's force and as the wood tore apart their fragments and splinters froze in midair—frozen in the mortal time-stream while the two supernatural beings sparred—and hung there as if mocking their lost weapons. Neither of them deterred, they darted through the bits of wood with their fists balled and ready. Two punches landed simultaneously and the room slipped back into normal time as the two were knocked out of overdrive and across the room until they came crashing down onto the unforgiving hardwood floor.

Zane groaned and rolled to his knees, struggling to stand up, and when he'd finally gotten to his feet, grabbing his shoulder in pain. Wincing from the contact, he glanced at the floor and let out a heavy sigh at the sight of the massive crack that he'd put there when he'd fallen; two perfect indents showing where his back and shoulders had broken through.

He silently thanked Gregori for his vast wealth and the assurance that the damage would be easily repaired.

The sound of metal straining caught his attention and he looked towards the opposite side of the room in time to see one of the weapon racks—loaded with a series of Oriental swords and daggers and cracked in half down the middle from Serena's fall—start to come unhinged. As he watched the collection of weapons start to shift, he watched as a short sword slipped free and stabbed into the floor several inches from Serena's head.

And the rest were sure to follow!

Growling, he fought through his own pain and dizziness and rushed towards her, pushing his already-drained body into overdrive and struggling to maintain the superhuman speed as the room slowed around him long enough for him to snatch her body from the floor and hurling them both out of range of the slew of razor-sharpness that rained down behind them.

Zane groaned and blinked against his worn-out body's blurring vision and saw Serena below him; pinned to the floor by his body.

Biting his lip at the compromising position, he hurried to pull himself off of her, hoping that she hadn't gotten the wrong idea or that he hadn't done any damage in falling on top of her. The sound of another crash reverberated in Zane's ears and he gritted his teeth as a second wave of falling weapons rang out and startled Serena into an upright position; holding her chest and coughing as she tried to catch her breath.

Zane sighed; at least she was safe.

He dropped his head to look at her, she was breathing softly and her chest lifted and fell in slow breaths. He chewed his lip as he realized he was staring at her chest still and turned his attention to her face. Her dark bluish-purple gaze was pulled into his and he frowned, realizing he'd been caught. She smirked and licked her lips. Realizing he was being teased, Zane looked away and growled.

"Like what you see?" she smirked.

"I was... I was just trying to help you; to *save* your dumb ass from getting sliced to shit!" He glared, "And, for the record, no. I *don't* like what I see! I prefer my women to have *tits*!"

Even filled with anger and embarrassment, his mismatched eyes were so beautiful. She'd caught him and he *knew* it; knew it and was *pissed* about it! She smiled to herself. She knew just how to get to him. Knew *exactly* what buttons to push.

Which worked to her benefit, because he was *hot* when he was angry.

While she'd known that her teasing would get him riled, she had not anticipated her own body's response to his piercing gaze.

Even then, in the midst of celebrating her own victory against his emotions, she felt tingles along the length of her arms at the memory of his stare.

Trying to move past her own thoughts, she dusted herself off and cleared her throat; "So what the hell happened, anyway?" she asked, motioning to the condition of the room.

"A lot…" He turned his attention and pulled back, "and the expensive kind of 'a lot', at that," he sighed, pushing his hair from his face.

She chuckled at all the damage and gave Zane a look, "Blah blah blah! I see my father's legacy lives on within you." She sighed and stretched out, shaking her head, "Bastard *always* bitched and moaned about cost! 'This costs this'! 'That costs that'!" She growled, "Just another reason why I left in the first place. It was *all* that the old man could talk about; the only thing I'm sure he *thought* about! Well, *one* of the only things at least," she added quietly.

Zane frowned and looked over at her, tilting his head as he thought for a moment. She was so different than most the girls he had met. Something about her that irritated and enticed all at once; an arrogance that bordered confidence—or was it the other way around?—and a perception that seemed to skew everything it took in.

He smiled softly; she was *definitely* a mystery to him.

And he'd always loved a good mystery.

"There's nothing wrong with being worried over finances, you know. Aside from you, everybody else seems to understand that much," he sighed and leaned against the wall to catch his breath, "And it's not like I *choose* to worry about it! Believe me, I'd much rather just have to worry about money. It'd be a lot more peaceful, I'm sure!"

Serena smirked, "Aw! Afraid you'll get more grey hairs?"

"It's *not* grey!" Zane growled, running the length of silver in his bangs between his fingers to analyze it himself, "And it's *not* from worrying, either!"

"So what is it from, Zane? More of this curse-thing? Just what *are* you?" She turned and sat next to him and leaned back as well, "You definitely aren't like any vampire or therion I've met before. I mean, I *saw* that… that *thing* you became, and I've never seen a therion look like that! But what sort of vampire can change its shape?"

"It's hard to say anymore. I sometimes feel like the vampire that dreamed he was a therion, other times I feel like the therion that dreamed he was a vampire." He looked down so that he wouldn't have to see her expression, "The only truth that matters is this: I'm a *real* monster. I'm what never should have been; what is supposed to be kept as nothing more than a myth or a threat—a boogieman for mythos parents to scare their kids into behaving. The point is to show me *real* suffering. It takes me when I'm at my most vulnerable and it leaves behind chaos with my name written all over it. It kills without discretion and it lives to destroy so that, when I'm back in control, I have to take in the aftermath and know it was me." He shook his head and sighed, "I'm a plague, Serena. A nuclear warhead handled by an idiot with a mallet. That's all you need to know."

"That's hard to believe," Serena drew her knees up and leaned against them for a moment. "I mean, you aren't a *bad* person—*sure*, you're a dick, and you definitely whine a lot—but that doesn't make you a monster. I can tell that much. Even if you *do* become some cheesy mythos version of The Hulk, I'd still think you were a pussy," she smirked, "but at least you're a pussy who's *also* a good person."

Zane scoffed and shook his head, "I *wish* I could become The Hulk! At least he's admired! I'm worse than what the comics could make me out to be… and besides, I'm not green." He looked over and smirked, though the smile didn't reach his eyes. Though she held his gaze briefly, he was forced to look away from her growing look of sympathy, wishing to everything he could believe in the words she was saying. Wishing he was something—*anything*—other than a monster. Leaning back until he faced the ceiling, he tried to stifle his body's shaking as the memories returned. He could still feel every puncture into his flesh; could still smell the ceremonial incense and boiling ink and spilled blood and putrid sweat and tears. He could still remember every agonizing second as the cursed ink assaulted and warped his body and core to a cellular and spiritual level. And every time he remembered, he felt the same scorching and his skin began to burn and crawl; trying to escape from itself and its history. "I should go." He went to stand up and walked towards the door before pausing and turning towards her, "You should go to the infirmary for some synth-blood if you're still in pain."

With that, he turned away from her and left the room.

"You like him, don't you?" Devon grumbled.

"He's a good person, I guess," Serena frowned and turned to Devon as he appeared beside her.

He sighed and she felt the warmth fill her more as he looked around the room.

"I can't protect you like this," his image shifted and faltered as he lost focus on staying visible. "Dammit, Serena, I'd give *anything* to be able to protect you like he can."

She turned to him and smiled warmly before standing up and walking over to him. "And you will, Devon. Soon enough! Sooner than you think! We'll find a body for you! This clan can help us both and when you're in your own body again we'll finally be able to be together! Just like we'd always planned! Forever!" She smiled and shook her head, "Don't worry about Zane! We aren't right for each other."

"If you say so," his spectral features curled into a smile and he chuckled, "Either way, I'm happy you said that," her aura shifted as he spoke, and he moved a palm that she couldn't feel over her cheek, "I love you, Serena."

She smiled, trying to hold back her emotions for his benefit. "I love you too, Devon."

Zane's eyes widened as he listened in to Serena's conversation. She was speaking to something—some*one*—else in the room, and though he couldn't *see* her aura he was certain that the shift in energy hadn't been somebody new. Either she was more out of her mind than he'd thought, or there was something occupying her auric force. Zane pried further, trying to figure out just what he was hearing without being seen. As he peeked around the corner he caught sight of her facing away from him, staring intently on whatever it was she was conversing with. As he narrowed his eyes in an attempt to see, something shifted in front of her—something shaped like a person, but completely transparent—as Serena's aura refracted some of the room's light. He frowned, wishing he could see auras in this body, but, sadly, that ability was reserved for the beast. Either way, one thing was for certain…

She wasn't crazy.

There was somebody anchored in her aura; somebody desperate enough to cling to another's life-force and still aware enough to carry on a conversation.

And an intimate one at that!

He frowned at the thought and, feeling a familiar tingle, looked down to see the tattoos on his arms glowing. Despite not wanting to hear any more of the one-sided ghostly conversation, he couldn't tune out Serena's words and he realized that he was the topic.

"We aren't right for each other."

He struggled to stifle a growl and shook his head as he turned away from the conversation to regain control. Why was he getting so upset?

It wasn't as though he'd thought any different.

He knew he was a monster and didn't deserve her.

Still, the burning in his chest was hard to argue with.

He'd already been forced to admit that with her around he felt more in tune with himself than ever before. Even the beast, which had *never* responded to *anybody* as something other than another thing to rip apart, seemed oddly calmed when she was near. And, selfish as it was, he wanted that peace to last.

He wanted her!

Swallowing away the feeling of nausea that crept inside of him and, after several deep breaths, looked down at his arm as it stopped shaking and the ink faded back to black. Knowing there was nothing more to be gained from eavesdropping than more pain he hurried away to the upper levels and into his room.

He couldn't trust her and, worse than that, he couldn't trust himself around her.

Zoey couldn't stand it!

Try as she might, she couldn't stay away from Isaac!

Though they both knew what they were doing was wrong, they had begun to see each other more often. She had sworn—taken what she'd hoped was a solid and unbreakable oath—to herself, for the benefit of her clan, never to see him again.

That oath had barely survived a day!

Damn him and his animal magnetism!

All inhibitions had been lost; all qualms and worries squelched and justified with flimsy reasoning.

It was wrong!

It was foolish!

It was reckless!

And Zoey loved it!

As the spark of excitement at being reacquainted with her forbidden lover was stoked to an all-consuming flame in her chest, she wove between the trees and hurdled stumps and rocks as they presented themselves. With Isaac keeping a steady pace beside her, she navigated through the forest, not caring where their journey took them. So long as she'd arrive there with him. She felt complete.

"You're too slow!" Isaac growled playfully as he sprinted ahead of her and cleared a gorge overlooking a shallow stream.

"No fair!" Zoey pouted, hurtling herself over the gap and, realizing she wouldn't close the distance, using her aura to carry her to the other side. As her feet touched down on the grass she let out a sigh of relief, keeping her eyes shut until she had caught her breath, "You're *used* to this sort of thing! You've been running in the woods your entire life!" She looked up to shoot him a glare and frowned when she saw that she was alone, "Isaac?"

She heard his laugh only a moment before he darted out of hiding and grabbed her by the waist and carried her deeper into the forest and up a hill with her holding onto his shoulders. His laughing carried as he ran with her, scaling the hill on bare feet as though it were nothing. As he planted his next step on a plot of earth, she gasped and cried out as the patch uprooted and he lost his footing. Pulling her into him, they rolled down the small, grassy slope together and finally landed on a patch of wildflowers that coughed pollen and petals into the air with the impact. As the evidence of their fall settled, Isaac, on his back below her, was still laughing.

"What's so funny?" she scolded, still breathless from the fall, "We could've died!"

"Nah. I know these hills too well to let them kill me," he smirked up at her, "Besides, I'm not easy to break."

She laughed, patting at his broad chest, "You, good sir, are a *beast!*"

His grin widened as he looked up at her as his eyes began to glow fiercely and he drew his face closer to hers. "I know I am. And you *love* it!" He caught her lips against his and she gasped softly, before closing her eyes and began kissing him back. She still wasn't used to the bestial passion in his kiss, which always caught her off guard no matter how prepared she was for it, but it only forced her to match his effort with her own to keep her head on her shoulders. She couldn't stop herself from succumbing to them each and every time, especially not when there was so much passion and sincerity behind them. She moaned as his hands skimmed her sides and he slowly began to pull away, leaving her lower lip with one final nip to remember him by.

As they fell back to share the view of the clear sky, they allowed themselves to get lost in their mutual emotions.

CHAPTER SEVEN
PLOTTING

Keith growled, staring at the haphazard batch of mythos sitting before him; a makeshift Council of his own design where he made the rules and called the shots.

And soon enough the *real* thing would be his, as well.

The table was abuzz with their collective plotting, and the murmurs between neighbors and the occasional rant from the others drew their attention inward as he stood at the head of the table. When they did not take notice of his gesture or silence their witless banter, he sneered. Shaking his head at their insubordination, he raised his arm over his head a moment before bringing his fist down on the table. The surface rocked and all of the eyes in the room widened and honed in on the source as one of the table's legs gave out and it sagged several inches to one side. As the last of the reverberation and emotional impact dissipated, the group leaned forward in their seats and awaited his plans.

He smirked. That, he noted with an approving nod, was how it *should* be!

After all, he *was* their leader!

"We will get nowhere if our efforts are not executed! A plan— no matter *how* perfectly designed—is *nothing* until it is put into action! I need commitment; I *demand* it! And I'm certain that I'm not alone in my desires to see something come of our efforts."

"Now, there is no doubt in my mind that the clan's moves will come sooner if we are not the first to attack." He grinned and turned to a marble chess set that adorned a shelf behind him, with a calculated movement, pinched the polished white king and queen pieces between his fingers and inspected them with a coy smirk before setting them on the table in front of the others to get a clear view. "You see, we are all *warriors* here; warriors who are *crippled* by those who would use us as nothing more than fodder!" He stabbed his index finger down at the king piece, "*They* would have you believe that—through their oppression and iron-grip on every detail of your lives—you were something *more* to them; using their condescending language and structurally unsound laws—upheld by a corrupt and biased police force that hide behind the veil of 'clan-hood' to justify the unjustifiable!—to control and bind us." He turned again and scooped up the pawns from the board, "And they would turn us—all of us!—into nothing more than drones!"—he began to roll each pawn across the uneven table's surface, allowing them to reach the end and fall to the floor—"Nothing more than expendable, faceless drones!" Growling, he held up the last pawn and rolled it between his fingers, "They would turn you into nothing more than *pawns* to be shuffled about their battlefields to protect those they deem worthy," he sneered at the piece and let it slip from his fingers to join the others on the floor. "I've *seen* them, my brothers! Seen them first-hand from my cushioned seat amongst their foul ranks, taking up arms against those too weak to defend themselves, and honoring the mundane needs of those who benefit and empower them!

"But now," he smirked and held his index finger over the king piece on the table, "there has been a shift"—he pulled his finger back, toppling the king and letting it roll off the table and clatter against the pawns—"and the army that would hold us back from claiming our rightful glory is without rule; without direction!"

Reaching behind him with his aura, he retrieved one of the white knights and let it sweep once over the heads of his audience before it landed beside the still-standing queen piece, "And all that stands between us and that glory is an ignorant queen and a broken knight." Again, he reached out with his aura, snatching up the remaining game pieces and letting them orbit his body as he jabbed an accusatory finger at the others, "And you *choose* to let this moment—this moment that you've waited your entire *lives* for!—be nothing more than pretty words on a sheet of paper that you call a *plan* that you're too afraid to put into action? And for what? So that you can *remain* their pawns? So that the comfort of ignorance can remain and the fear of change can be avoided?

"Gentlemen," he let the word slip from his tongue like a vulgar, oily thing, "it is time to free yourselves from their tyranny; to stop playing along with their silly games." The floating pieces fell, one-by-one, from the air until only a white rook and a black knight remained. As the others watched, he took these into his palm and smirked. "In their weakened state, we can *take* their castle as our own"—he slammed the rook down in front of him—"and you can finally be free of your lives as pawns"—he held up the black knight and nodded slowly at it—"and claim the 'warrior' title that's always been yours!"

With that, he slammed the knight between the white queen and knight, letting both collapse and roll off of the table, leaving only the black knight and the white rook standing. The others stared for a moment, taking in the sight of the coal-black horse that stared angrily at the bone-white castle set out in front of it, and their grins widened.

Seeing that he'd made his point, Keith smiled and sat down, steepling his fingers in front of him. "Checkmate."

"What do you propose we do next then?" an older vampire leaned forward, "Like you've said, The Council *is* starting to get wind of our motives."

"You leave that to me," Keith bowed his head once, "Don't worry about that detail. The clan and The Council will not be an issue anymore. On that you have my word. Now, if you'll excuse me," he stood and started for the door, "I have other business to attend to."

With that, he disappeared from the group, jumping into overdrive and seeking out his next target. Finally, sensing he was close, he allowed himself to drop out of his superhuman speed and came to stand in the forest. The overpowering stench of body odor and wet animal fur assaulted his senses and he sneered at the smell of the Therions. They *really* were just a bunch of beasts; only slightly more clever than the pathetic creatures they shared the features of. Still, they served their purposes.

Even if they weren't fully aware of what that purpose was.

He sensed the pack's leader as he stepped towards him from the side and he smirked. "Having fun, Isaac?" he glanced over and shook his head, clucking his tongue, "My my... a *vampire*, eh? Is she as good as she looks?"

"Leave her out of this!" he snarled, stepping towards him before adding, "And leave *us* out of this."

"Oh no, my friend! I am *far* from being done with you and yours! You see, The Council has put a call out on the Clan of Vail. It seems that those of my blood are lacking in family values, and I need your pack to take them out. All of them," he smirked, "*including* your little auric girlfriend."

Isaac snarled and shook his head, clenching his fists and preparing to attack, "My pack has done plenty for The Council! We will have no more of your orders!" He growled again and his skin started shifting in response to his anger as he advanced another step.

"I'm not presenting this as a choice, therion! This is a *command*, and if you refuse a command from The Council—*The* Council that *you're* sworn to obey—then your pack will suffer the consequences of your decision," Isaac roared and lunged at Keith, who laughed and dodged the attack before pinning the therion against a nearby tree and extending his fangs.

"I would like nothing more than a reason, dog! Give me that reason, and I will do this my way, by killing you and *taking* your pack by force! It was a courtesy to ask you nicely, but clearly my hospitality is not appreciated. If you still want to defy us, I ask that you not waste any more of my time. I am, after all, in the middle of planning my next move."

"Th-then mo… move… to Hell!"

Keith tightened his grip. "Care to repeat that?" he snarled. "I will not ask again, Isaac! Either you obey or you die! Now are you going to do as I say?"

"Y-yes…" Isaac growled in defeat, still struggling to breath past Keith's grip.

"Good dog," Keith stepped back and let him drop, "You earned yourself a biscuit," he snickered at his own joke and turned away, "*Au revoir*, Rover!"

The bastard vampire disappeared, followed shortly after by his greasy, synthetic stink, and Isaac let his shoulders sag once he was certain that he wasn't being watched. Feeling suddenly very exhausted, he leaned against the nearby tree and tried to clear his head. He didn't want to condemn his pack—his *family*—to any more chaos, and he didn't know if he could ensure their safety if it meant going against Zoey, perhaps even *killing* her…

Though it had only been a short time, he couldn't bring

himself to do anything that would cause her harm.

He shuddered at the thought and cupped his hand over his heavy eyes, trying to massage away a growing headache.

"Hey, Isaac!" Zoey's voice chimed from a short distance away, "You alright?"

He dropped his hand and sighed, "Yeah, I'm fine. Just fine."

"No, you're not." She stepped towards him, her stride filled with more confidence and purpose than he was used to seeing from her, "Tell me what's wrong!" She walked around him as he tried to turn his back to her, her unrelenting blue eyes filled with determination and worry for him as she placed her hand on his cheek.

He growled and turned his face away from her touch; not feeling worthy of it after considering Keith's offer. He wasn't sure he ever would again. And yet, when he turned his face back to hers, drawn in by his own needs, all he could see was the hurt in her eyes, and he saw that it didn't matter *what* he did. Either way she would be forced to suffer for his choice. He bit his lip and looked down, not wanting to make the decision.

Not now...

Not ever!

"Please! I told you I'll be okay, Zoey."

"No, you said you *were* okay! So what's all this talk of *going* to be okay?" she frowned, shaking her head, "Isaac... please."

He sighed and put his hands on her shoulders. For her it would seem like a reassuring gesture, but the reality was that it was a simple way to keep her held back. "You should go home to your clan for the night. They'll be worried, and we can't afford to be found out. Not like this."

"Why won't you tell me? I thought..." She shook her head, tears welling in her eyes, "Please don't do this!" She shot him a sudden glare, "I don't *want* to have to go into your head and find out for myself! But if you won't tell me then you leave me with no—"

He frowned, he couldn't keep her and he sure as hell didn't

want to hurt her anymore, but if he didn't get her to leave—get her to stay away from him *and* his secret—then both they *and* their comrades would be in danger. He shook his head and let out a small growl as he turned his shifting eyes to hers, hoping the bestial glare and animal sound would be enough to sway her. "*There's* a surprise," he spat, baring his teeth as they shifted in his skull, "A *vampire* being a leech!" He sneered, "You think I'd tell you *anything?*" Scoffing, he shook his head and turned away so she wouldn't see his tortured features. Knowing that his aura would give him away, he focused on the rage he had for Keith and hoped it would provide the same effect. "We are enemies! We were *never* meant to be together! You were just convenient; a toy for me to pass the time! And though it was fun while it lasted, Zoey, I've gotten bored. Playtime is over! Now go home!"

The air went suddenly cold and Isaac had to force himself not to look. Zoey was strong, there was no doubting that, and if she was responsible for the drop in temperature than it was obvious he'd struck a nerve. "You're lying," she growled, the air around him kicking up his hair and throwing it in his face, "You think you can *hide* it from me? I can tell; even *without* looking I can tell! I know we're enemies, Isaac, I know we shouldn't be together! But that doesn't matter; not to *either* of us! When I'm with you, I feel right! I don't care about this war or what I'm supposed to feel! I don't even care what the others at the clan would think! For once in my life I'm being selfish and—dammit, Isaac!—I want to be with you!"

Isaac stared at her, blinking against the wave of fury and passion that had just been dumped on him. Biting his lip, he frowned as he struggled to keep his eyes on hers, trying to figure out what she was thinking.

"Fuck," he sighed and shook his head, feeling his own expression betray his attempts to drive her away, "What am I going to do with you?"

"Well, you still need to earn my forgiveness for what you said," she said, "So you might want to start by kissing me."

He grinned and licked his lips, "With pleasure."

Hooking his hand behind her head, he pulled her face to his and pressed his lips to hers with all the ferocity of a predator finding a meal. She moaned against his mouth, driving him to pull her closer to his body until the space between them was nothing but a vulgar memory. Her body fit his *perfectly!* Every contour and every crevice seemed to exist to allow the other to occupy it. She whimpered as he ran his hands across her sides, tracing her form with his palms. Using his wandering hands and her small body to his advantage, he lifted her easily from her feet and pulled her body on top of him.

"O-oh! Isaac!" She blushed.

Blushing, but *not* complaining; not struggling or resisting or rejecting.

With that, they both held on tight to the other as they joined in the bliss of the night.

Their forbidden embrace holding them strong.

Isaac yawned as he woke up on the forest floor, finding himself tangled with Zoey's still-sleeping body. He smiled warmly and worked on unraveling their limbs and set her gently against the tree as he stood up and walked to the nearby lake to get a drink.

"So good to see that my demands haven't swayed your interest in that vampire bitch! I hope that…" He scoffed, "… *acquainting* yourself with her body won't prove to be distracting in the long run," Keith's mocking voice called from behind him.

"Get out of here! I already said I wasn't going help you anymore and I meant it!" Isaac growled and turned to face him as his body began to shift.

"Oh I don't think so, Isaac! I'm not done with you yet!" Keith grinned and stepped forward. As Isaac focused to transform his body he suddenly felt himself gripped in an invisible force that began to crush him. Unable to fight against the force of Keith's aura as it squeezed tighter and began to weave more and more through his body and mind, he cried out in agony. "You and your pack *will* fight for me! There is no other option for you!" He smirked and stepped closer, "You see, I don't need *you* to make the order; I just need your body! And, as I'm sure you're beginning to realize, your body is very, *very* easily controlled. Now, you can choose to play along and do as you're told, or I can hollow out your head and *make* you do as you're told! The outcome, either way, is the same, but I'm sure you'd rather not let me have all the fun, am I right?"

Isaac growled and, despite the pain, glared at him, "You couldn't control me if you—"

Keith glared, "Am. I. Right?" He tightened his aura's hold on the therion and began to pry into his mind, unlocking all the barriers and restraints in Isaac's mind until…

Isaac settled, no longer struggling or snarling. "Yes, Keith. Quite right, indeed."

"That's a good boy!" Keith smiled at his own success and chuckled as he set Isaac down. "Now be off! There's work to be done!"

"Yes. Of course," Isaac bowed his head and started towards his pack.

Watching the therion disappear into the forest, Keith nodded to himself. The plan was coming together beautifully! Now there was just the simple business of Vail's takeover. Satisfied that his work in the woods was finally done and he could be free of it, he turned away and started towards the city.

"Time for a family reunion, sis."

CHAPTER EIGHT
COLLAPSE

SERENA SIGHED BEHIND THE FAR-too-fancy desk in the far-too-large room she had been given by her far-too-hospitable clan. Everything, the whole "welcome back, princess, oh how you've been missed"-scene that everybody—even those who hadn't been with Vail long enough to even *remember* her—seemed to be playing by, felt forced. Just a synthetic comfort. No different than the fake blood they all gleefully guzzled down just because it rid them of the guilt of tapping a *real* vein for sustenance.

And so there she sat.

Alone in a sea of scripted loyalty...

… behind a still-too-fancy desk!

"Goddam thing's bigger than my *cabin!*" She grumbled, casting an accusing glare at the massive portion of polished mahogany that was partially hidden under the old letters that Zane had offered her several days earlier after their chat in the infirmary.

Several days…

And already the tides of the calm-though-scripted sea were beginning to shift.

In only a few days Zane had become nearly non-existent, growing evermore distant with each passing day. Furthermore, in that same time, Zoey had become scarce around the clan's headquarters, and any time that she *was* around she seemed to be distracted; lost in her own world and leaving Serena behind in the gloom of reality to rot behind a desk.

A god-damned, stupid, worthless desk!

Groaning, she looked down at the letters that her father had been keeping before his death once more and deciphering, as she had each and every time she offered the pages her attention, *nothing* from them! Tapping her index finger against the wood—hoping that, maybe, she could "accidentally" gouge a piece and put some personality on the desktop—and frowned at another batch of guilt that grew in her mind like an ivy that throttled the life out of every other thought she had. Despite her many years of convincing herself otherwise, she could no longer blame her father for what had happened. It had never been Gregori's fault. Not really! Rather, it had just been a series of shitty circumstances that she'd blamed on him; the easiest target to project her personal need for a source to all of it. She sighed, wishing again that she could've had the chance to apologize to the bastard before he was killed.

Zane had explained that her father's death had been Keith's doing, and there was no doubt at this point that he was *also* their mother's murderer. And, with all this new knowledge—this new knowledge that had been thrown into the spotlight—she had absolutely *no* idea what to do or where to begin. Instead, as she took her head into her hands and, trying to control her jagged breaths, she focused on a far simpler and far more pressing task:

"Do. Not. Cry!" She whispered to herself, "Not even one goddam tear or I will—"

Are you about to threaten yourself for wanting to cry? Devon's voice chimed behind her as his warmth encompassed her. *You know that it's okay to cry, right? Just like those cheesy after-school specials preach; 'don't bottle it in' and all that jazz.*

She faked a smile, wishing that she could lean against him but knowing she'd only find warm air where there should have been flesh. Sighing, she looked down sadly and tapped harder at the desk.

Don't worry so much! It's like you said, we'll find a body soon. Devon said.

"I hope so," she sighed, "But at least I'm not finding my own food, right?"

He nodded. Devon had always had a distaste for her feeding on humans, so being in the clan, where she was supplied with all the "blood"—if she could *really* call it that—she needed, must have been a relief to him. Smiling at his reaction, she found herself wondering if Zane felt that same way about their feeding habits, but quickly shook those thoughts away.

What's on your mi— Devon started to ask before suddenly disappearing, along with the warmth and his ghostly influence on her aura.

Startled by the sudden silence, Serena started to call out to him but stopped when she heard laughing from the door.

Growling, she turned towards the door and positioned her hands out as her aura shifted into the shape of a bow in her grip, holding it at the ready for the intruder on the other side. With the laughter growing clearer, an auric beam appeared in the middle of her "weapon" and she drew it back like an arrow—following the movements and habits from her archery training—and leveled it at the door.

"Get out of here, Keith!" She shouted.

"Oh my! Ouch! Is that the greeting I deserve, my dear sister!

No hugs or tears of joy to see your long lost brother?" Keith smirked.

"Go to Hell, you prick! You haven't been lost nearly long enough!" She growled as she 'fired' at him.

Side-stepping the purple beam of light as it collided with the wall, Keith smirked. "Hmm, tempting! But I'd rather not." His own, stronger aura shot out and grabbed her own as she moved to retrieve the "arrow". "However," he laughed as he held out his hand and an auric bolt of his own shot back at her and slammed into her chest, "since you seem so taken with the place, you're welcome to take my place!"

The force of the impact knocked the wind from Serena's lungs and the ground from beneath her feet, and she cried out as she fell back before everything turned black.

Smoke was already filling the entire building as Zane rushed through the halls, slamming on every door he passed and warning others to head to the main hall for evacuation instructions. The panic in the halls was becoming stifling, and even without an aura he could feel the combined energies making the hazy air crackle. Finally, he reached Serena's room and, not about to waste any time, kicked in the door and growled as a cloud of smoke poured from the opening and into his face.

"Serena? Serena!" he rushed in and began scanning the room through burning eyes, "God-fucking-dammit! Serena! Answer me!"

A short ways to his left a breathy cough and a stifled whimper sounded and he honed in on it, starting towards the source.

Then the beast called.

Crying out in pain as he tried to hold it back, his vision turned red and fell to the floor; Serena still unconscious several feet from him. Reaching out to pull her to him, he cringed as the bones in his arms began to fracture and lengthen all at once. Trying to pull himself together to reach Gregori's daughter, he shrieked out in pain as his back lurched forward. He growled, seething in pain as he continued to fight to get to Serena. If she was truly special—if the beast saw *anything* in her that would give him the chance to force it to stop—then he *had* to reach her.

Both of their lives depended on it!

"G-god damn you!" he gritted against the pain as he struggled to fight the change, "I... I *know* you can f-f-fucking hear us!" he growled and shook his head, "*Me*! You *can* hear me! You can hear—AHH! Shit!—hear me... and you sure as shit can understand!" Trying to ignore the violent shift of his organs he fought to crawl closer, "And... I *swear* on everything I hold sacred; if you allow her to die then I'm going after her!" the change slowed and the pain numbed. He smirked through his agony and nodded, "Y-yea? Don't like *that*, huh? Not having a body put a damper on your fucking plans? Try to see how much death and destruction you bring as fucking *worm food*, you dumb bastard! You *need* me and *we* need *her*! Now... let... me... GO!"

The pain hit him like a semi-truck and knocked him to the floor. Every centimeter of his body burned and ached and throbbed as everything shifted at once.

And all he could do was smile.

"Th-thank you!" Though it was excruciating, he could feel his body shifting back; the beast working overtime to put him back together fast enough to save her! Nodding as the torture subsided, he pulled himself up, "We'll settle this later, asshole!"

With nothing left to hold him back, he rushed forward and scooped Serena's body from the floor with ease before retreating back into the halls to escape the growing flames.

As he turned a corner and broke through a curtain of fire he was met head-on by a massive creature as it lunged at him. Before he could react, both of them were thrown back and through the wall behind them. Zane roared as the layers of mortar and plywood and wiring shattered and snapped around him as he struggled to protect Serena's body in the process.

She couldn't be injured!

She wouldn't be injured!

They would be sure of it!

"I won't—" he snarled as they crashed to the floor on the other side of the wall and the world went redder and hotter. "W-we…" He smirked and set Serena down carefully—making sure to keep her out of his and the therion's range—and nodded to himself, finally allowing the pain to come, *"WE WILL NOT LET YOU HURT HER!"*

The change came all at once, hitting him out of a mutual need rather than simply wanting to see him suffer from prolonged agony. One moment he was in Hell—howling and cursing in agony—and the next they were whole.

Perfect!

The therion that had caught him off guard huffed angrily at the sight of them on the other side of the wall and sprinted on all fours towards them. Seeing their opponent's reaction, a mouth far-too-big for its face curled up in an amused sneer that tickled the lobes of their misshapen ears, and they ran a long, narrow tongue over the bottom row of razor-sharp fangs. Catching sight of this, the therion's face shifted—its once confident dark-orange aura recoiling as fear settled in—and it halted in mid-stride to rethink its approach.

But there *was* no other option for it.

No choice that wouldn't ultimately lead to the same outcome.

"DEATH!" They cackled and leapt through the hole they'd made in their previous form.

The therion's eyes went wide and it scrambled to turn in the narrow hall and flee only to have them come down on its back; a talon from one foot slamming down and hooking the vertebrae of the whimpering therion's spine.

As they relished in the succulent cocktail of terror and pain that rolled from their prey in great waves, a shiver coursed through their body and their scarlet aura shot from their chest and ensnared the therion. Retracting the talon and stepping down, they hoisted the massive mythos into the air to face them in all their glory; that it might know—when it landed in Hell—what *not* to fuck with!

"YOU WERE WRONG TO PISS HIM OFF, MUTT!" They cackled, running a clawed hand across the therion's sternum and letting its life gush down its torso and flow in torrents to their feet, *"BUT WE ARE VERY GLAD THAT YOU DID! NEVER BEFORE HAS HE LET US OUT SO FREELY!"* They wet their black lips before extending their tongue and dipping it into the gaping wound in its chest. They moaned as their enemy's life-force flowed into their mouth, and the light spectrum shifted momentarily as their eyes reacted to the energy. *"OH YES! VERY GLAD, INDEED!"*

The therion whimpered again, trying to struggle against them, its aura sagging more and more as its death became a certainty.

"WE HOPE YOU'LL UNDERSTAND," they came down with their claws once again, taking the front half of the therion's face off and letting it slam wetly into the wall before leaving a trail to the floor, *"IT'S JUST BUSINESS!"*

Zoey was certain that she hadn't blinked her eyes once since waking up alone on the forest floor to the smell of smoke and the psychic cries of her clan-mates. The journey from the woods was torturous, each step bringing her that much closer to an already agonizing truth that she wanted so desperately to prove false. Isaac's absence and her clan's attack couldn't be a coincidence—not with how he'd been acting the night before—and she had *ignored* every sign just so she could…

She choked on a sob that was soon-after drowned out by the howling of sirens.

As a fire truck shot by—flashing lights and blaring wails warning any in its path to move aside—she threw out her aura and hooked it. As her psychic tether pulled her off her feet, she drew herself in until she was able to grab hold of the roof-mounted ladder and hitched a ride with the EMT caravan to whatever remained of the Vail Clan's headquarters.

Though it seemed like hours, the truck came to a screeching halt in front of the building only minutes later, and as the crew began to flood from the vehicle, Zoey threw her aura out and carried herself to a ledge on the third-floor and snuck in through a window.

The elevators were already out of service in response to the fire, and the shriek of the building's alarm made any sort of clear thought as to *how* to get underground difficult. Finally, fed up with logic and calculations, she opted for the more Zane-like approach and tore the elevator doors from the wall and lifted the cab out of her way to open up a straight drop in the shaft.

Like an Olympic diver, she hurled herself over the platform and into the plunging depths of the pitch-black elevator shaft; relying solely on her aura to gauge the distance to the bottom. As she plummeted in a nosedive, she threw out several auric tendrils and began ripping each level's door free from the wall, positive that their escape would be hindered if they were forced to clear them on the way out.

With the bottom fast approaching, Zoey focused her aura into three sections and secured a hold in the shaft as a fourth tendril shot out and broke through the passage to their clan's lobby. Using the auric slingshot she'd set herself into, she launched herself through, using the momentum and added force to catapult herself into the depths of the inferno and following after the familiar auric signals of her friends.

It wasn't hard to find them.

Zane had already transformed and was dripping in the blood of more therions than she cared to guess. Scanning the area, she "saw" Serena, unconscious and badly beaten, in a room on the other side of the hall and she started towards it before coming across Zane's handiwork.

Bits and pieces of his previous opponents—still wearing the color and claw of their bestial forms—littered the bloodied hall and adding the stink of blood to the lingering traces of agony and terror left behind. Her eyes took in the aftermath of her friend's onslaught before coming to rest on him as he squared-off against another therion.

One with an all-too-familiar aura…

Her eyes widened, "Isaac!"

A myriad of questions went through her head as she watched the two circling one another, searching for an opening to rip through.

Had Isaac been planning this the entire time?

Was his affection for her *really* just an act?

Was he responsible for whatever had happened to Serena?

And, probably the most burning question of all:

Did she care if Zane ripped him apart?

She shook her head, again abandoning the burden of thought and rolling on pure instinct, and went to rush towards the two. An angry and tortured shriek tore past her lips as she approached, causing the two to shift their gazes at whoever was *crazy* enough to come between their death match. Seeing Zoey coming at him, Isaac turned his body to face her; his usually fierce and intense eyes now glassy and dull. Zoey stopped several feet in front of him and frowned at the empty expression—no sense of recognition or familiarity; neither love nor hatred to give away his motives—that he gave to her.

There was *nothing* of him in those eyes.

Trapped in the dead orbs, Zoey wasn't aware of the newcomer until their guttural growl echoed through the hall and up her spine. Daring to look away from Isaac and towards the sound, she saw that another therion—aura boiling over with rage from the evidence of its allies' deaths surrounding it—that zeroed its sights on her and started a mad-dash in her direction.

It couldn't see the vacancy in Isaac's eyes.

It couldn't see the concern in hers.

It only saw what it wanted to see: a vampire standing in front of its leader amidst the strewn body parts of countless other therions.

She cried out and took a step away from the approaching threat. "Isaac!"

But he didn't respond; didn't even bat an eyelash as the other therion grabbed her by the throat and pinned her against the wall, snarling as it pulled back its opposite hand for the killing blow.

Seeing this, Zane let out a furious bellow and grabbed her attacker's shoulder to pull it back. Dead-set on Zoey's death, the therion blindly rolled its shoulder free and threw Zane back. He crashed into the ground and growled as he lifted himself up again.

They were down, but they were most certainly *not* out of the fight!

But the filthy dog's efforts *had* bought it enough of an opening to slaughter Zoey before they could get to them. As its claws came down at the screaming Zoey, their eyes widened to take in the horrific yet enticing sight of the impending death.

But it didn't come.

The other dog—the one they'd been ready to maim moments earlier—suddenly seemed to have a change of heart and held his comrade's arm only several inches from Zoey's face, bearing his fangs at him as a warning before pulling him away from her and shoving him down the hall, not shifting his gaze until the other was gone.

Zoey looked up at her unlikely savior, her eyes shimmering with an expression they didn't understand. "Isaac!"

The therion grunted and puffed its chest, but made no move to attack her.

Their eyes narrowed at the two as the scene unfolded. *"YOU KNOW THIS MONSTER?"*

Zoey looked at them and shook her head, "Zane! You don't understand! He was being contro—"

Snarling, they stepped towards the two. Their scarlet aura whipped free and slashed at the walls, raining down debris on all of them. *"WHAT HAVE YOU DONE? LOOK AT WHAT THEY—"*

"Enough!" Zoey glared at them and threw her sea-blue aura out and pinned them against the wall, "This is *hardly* the time for me to have to explain to you when you're like *this!*" She closed the distance between them and slapped her hand on their side with enough force to drive her point.

And then they were tired.

So very, very tired...

Zane groaned, slumping to the floor as a nauseating dizziness turned the world on its side. In the distance—off in the real world, far from the haze he was trapped within—he could feel his body shifting and tugging; hearing the *pops* and *snaps* of a body doing what it was never meant to do:

Become something else.

As the sounds and sensations faded, so did his grogginess, until he finally felt secure enough in the world to sit up without fear of slipping into orbit. As he'd suspected, his body was once again his own. He blinked at the sight of his own fingers before looking up at Zoey and the therion. Luckily, his pants hadn't been ripped too badly and, by some miracle that seemed only to work in comic books, were able to stay on.

"Y-you're getting *too* good at that," he shook his head at Zoey and sighed, "And wasn't this place on *fire* a second ago?"

Zoey shrugged, "I put them out."

"You can do that?"

Another shrug, "No oxygen, no fire. All I had to do was—"

"You know what," Zane held up a hand to stop her, "I just remembered that I have a headache and your big words won't help that. Straight to the point; fire is gone! Now, more importantly:"— he turned his attention to the therion and glared—"*who* is this and *why* am I not killing him?"

Zoey bit her lip and glanced up at him before looking away again, "He's..." She blushed, keeping her gaze down.

The therion whimpered and Zane almost thought he saw the

creature blush.

Zane shook his head and sneered, "It doesn't matter, either way! They are our *enemies*!" He glared, "Or have you already forgotten about Grego—"

"Gregori's death had *nothing* to do with them *or* their kind!" Zoey snapped. "Like it or not—despite all his wonderful qualities—he *was* an old and bigoted vampire with a vendetta against *anybody* that wasn't a vampire! We're at the cusp of a new chapter for this clan, and I suggest you shed all the unnecessary prejudices he taught you before they poison us any further!" She looked back at the therion and gave him a slight nod and watched as he started to change back. "Besides, Zane, we have the *same* enemy, and they can help us fight!" She shook her head angrily, "Assuming you didn't *kill* all of them!"

Even the therion, still in the middle of his transformation, looked surprised at her outburst.

Zane scoffed, "Our enemy? *Helping* us?"

She had a determined look in her face, "It was *Keith*! He's been manipulating them from the *start*! He was controlling Isaac—using him to give his pack commands against his will—until"—she blushed and looked at him—"he saw I was in danger." She sighed, "Look, I can't blame you for this—none of us can!—just like you can't blame them! We've *both* lost allies because of Keith! They deserve a chance to avenge their own... and besides, we could use the help. Even *you* can't deny *that*!"

"What I can't deny," Zane said with a disgusted sneer, "is that your boyfriend had better find some place to hide *that* thing!"

Zoey frowned and followed his gaze to Isaac's rapidly changing body and turned bright red as she realized that he had no clothes.

"Seriously! I'm willing to let bygones be bygones if you'll tell Babe Ruth here to put away the slugger before he puts somebody's eye out!"

The therion finished his transformation, his skin tightening around his lean frame as several of his ribs noticeably shifted into place. Ignoring Zane's remark and making no move to cover himself, he took in the carnage around him.

"Keith will suffer for every one of them!" he swore under his breath

"I'm suffering here and now, wild stallion! You want to put that thing in a stable so we can talk like civilized—"

Isaac glared, "Nobody's asking you to look!"

"Oh, right!" Zane rolled his eyes, "Let's try *not* to notice it! I'm surprised it hasn't tried to bite me!"

Zoey blushed and stepped in front of him, "I'll… uh, find him something to wear."

"Please do," Zane sighed, "And I'll try *real* hard not to ask how you're still walking."

The auric's already bright-red face blossomed with another flush of color and she started to herd the still-glaring therion down the hall.

"Send out a call to any survivors to meet us on the roof, if we're going to work together than we might as well do it right." He sighed and looked off towards the hole at the end of the hall and started towards it, hoping Serena hadn't taken a turn for the worse, "And make it fast! This place looks ready to come down and I don't want to be in it when it does!"

Stepping through the opening, he approached Serena's unconscious body and lifted her easily and started towards the lobby to wait for Zoey. While he hated the idea of abandoning the clan's headquarters—even more than how much he hated the idea of trusting a pack of therions to keep him alive—he couldn't deny that it was the only option.

"C'mon, Serena," he sighed, looking down at her face, "Let's get out of here!"

CHAPTER NINE
DEPTHS

THE RAGTAG GROUP OF SURVIVORS—composed of the vampires of the clan lucky enough to survive the fire and the therions of Isaac's pack fortunate enough to have survived Zane— were able to flee the building. Utilizing a psychic cloak that Zoey and the other aurics had put around them to avoid being seen by the slew of humans that had begun arguing amongst themselves over *how* a fire of such magnitude could magically squelch itself. Though they were able to avoid being detected, the combined force of the auras was not able to shade them from the sun, and the sang vampires, who were far more sensitive to the sun's radiation than any of the others, soon became restless and agitated.

Including Zane.

"Shit! Where the hell will we go now?" Serena frowned, her own skin beginning to itch under the UV assault.

"The only fucking place we have left!" Zane growled, glaring at Serena and growling when she glared right back at him. Finally, seeing that neither of them was about to back down from the other, he looked away, "Gregori had a backup plan for *everything*! Global battle, invasion, natural disaster... fuck, even *Z-Day* was considered!"

Zoey frowned, "Z-day?"

"Not now, Zoey!" Zane snapped at the skeptic tone, "The *point* is that he was prepared! And, given the shit we've found ourselves in, I'd say that what we need most is a place to hide and prepare!"

"Prepare for *what*?" a young blond sang trailing behind spat. Though he wasn't of age to be a warrior, his brashness made it clear that he was eager, and, while Zane admired his tenacity, he was hardly in the mood for his attitude. "Our leader's *dead*, our home has been *destroyed*, our clan has been reduced to a *joke*, and we're planning on a full-scale attack on a *Council* member with the help of a bunch of ass-sniffing *dogs*! What is there to plan, huh? Who shoots who first? 'Cuz if *you're* the best we got, then I'd rather take the bullet right here, right now!"

Zane's eyes shifted back towards him and his fangs extended as his rage grew, "Don't tempt us, boy! I don't have the time *or* the patience to deal with your shit and I've got *more* than enough ways to kill you and twice as many reasons to do so, but I'm hardly the one you should be watching out for."

"Oh yea, tough guy? And *who* should I be watching out for?"

Zane smirked wickedly, "The ass-sniffing dogs. See, where *I'm* trained in a number of ways to kill you before you'd even *know* it; they've lived in the wild their whole lives; surviving by using tooth and claw to take apart anything that threatened that survival. So, you arrogant little shit, while you might not care if I end you with your dignity intact, I suggest you watch your fucking mouth around the ones that would tear you open and rape your insides with the sort of equipment whales would envy."

The young sang stayed quiet.

Serena sighed and shook her head, "Dick!"

Zane smirked and nodded, "Exactly!" As they approached the outskirts of town and into the shady canopy of trees the sangs of the group let out a simultaneous sigh of relief, "Anyway! Though Gregori *hated* the wilderness"—he glanced back at the therions—"even though there's *nothing* wrong with it; he *also* knew that many others shared his distaste. So, in the event of a takeover and the need to retreat to someplace less obvious and more secluded, he had this built."

Stopping beside a large boulder, he smirked and laid his hand against its jagged surface.

Serena raised an eyebrow. "My father built a *rock*?"

Zoey was unable to stifle her laughter as Zane's face sagged. When her bout of hysteria had died down to something more manageable, she gave Zane an apologetic—albeit insincere—look.

"Not just *any* rock, Serena," she smiled as her aura emerged and wrapped around the boulder, lifting it and moving it several feet to one side, "A rock that hides the entrance to a reserve base!"

Serena frowned, noticing a perfectly-squared section of the ground that sunk in slightly. As she watched, Zane kicked some of the excess soil from its surface and, in doing so, uncovered a metal grate. Crouching down, Zane pried open a panel and revealed a keypad like the one Serena had seen him use in the clan's elevator to access their base. Following the pattern he had before, the grate soon groaned as something on the other side shifted and allowed him to pull it open.

"My father built a second base in a *hole*?" Serena frowned, peeking over his shoulder at the tunnel that stretched beyond her range of vision into the depths. She frowned, noticing a series of polished metal rungs that served as a ladder for anybody crazy enough to *want* to go in, "Couldn't he have at least put an elevator or something in this one?"

Zane shook his head. "It was hard enough to build *this* without being noticed. Too much construction would've gotten unwanted attention, so we had to skimp on a few of the more luxurious accommodations," he sneered up at her, "So I'm afraid your royal Jacuzzi will have to wait."

"Or I can just cut you open and have me a Bathory moment," Serena stuck her tongue out.

Zoey laughed again.

Zane divided his glare between the two of them, "Are you done yet?"

Serena chuckled, "Far from it, grouchy-pants, but I think I'll save the rest for when I've seen just what it is my father built that you're so defensive about." Though she tried her best not to show it, a lump formed in her gut as she stepped pass Zane and started to descend the ladder into the artificially lit tunnel. Zane growled, the sound echoing past Serena and making her all the more proud of being the cause of it. "Aren't you coming? After your lovely description I'd imagine you'd be more excited to hunker down in your precious *hole* in the *ground*!" She heard Zane grumble something inaudible and it was a moment before she realized he was talking to Zoey. "What was that?"

"Nothing! Now hurry up!" Zane started after her as the others followed.

"He said he wishes he could lay you in a hole in the ground!" Zoey laughed and stepped in after them, pulling the grate shut behind her and lingering for a moment as her aura reached out.

Serena frowned, confused, before she cringed at the sudden rumble as the boulder that had been hiding the entrance was dragged back into place.

"I didn't say *lay* her! I said *put* her in a hole! As in six-feet unde—"

Zoey giggled, "Not how I heard it."

Isaac growled, "Can we move a little faster? Some of us aren't used to small places!"

Zane nodded, looking glad to have something else to focus on, and motioned for Serena to continue.

"Zoey, get Isaac and his pack mates some fresh clothes while I get the other generators running. We don't have too many rooms, so we'll have to pair up and decide where everyone's sleeping," Zane instructed.

Nodding, Zoey motioned for Isaac and the others to follow as she started down one of the four corridors that shot off from the circular lobby that the ladder had led them into. A series of fluorescent lighting fixtures adorned the ceiling and the tunnels, and Serena took these in with a frown.

"Who turned on the lights?"

Zane led her down one of the other tunnels, "I did. When I opened the door one of our smaller generators turned on to provide enough light until we could manually turn on the others."

"Others?"

Zane nodded, "Mmhm. This whole place runs on energy provided by a bunch of generators. *Most* of them are like giant, magic batteries—ones that were charged with power from some of Vail's aurics and store that power until we need it. But, as I'd said, your dad was always prepared with a plan-B. So he *also* put in a set of generators that store solar energy."

Serena cocked an eyebrow, "Are you serious? *Solar* energy?"

"Yea yea, I thought it was ironic, too," he chuckled, "Creatures of darkness going green and using the sun for power and whatnot. But, in the long run, it was the best way to ensure that we'd have a reserve if the auric batteries died out."

"The auric batteries can die?"

Zane nodded as he stepped up to a series of consoles and began turning on the monitors. "Sure can. Everything dies eventually. Leave a battery out too long and the energy begins to fade. It might take hundreds and hundreds of years for it to happen, but we were never sure *when* or even *if* we'd have to use this place."

Serena shook her head, "So what was my father's plan if the *sun* died?"

"If the sun died"—he gave her a condescending look—"then we wouldn't be having his conversation."

"Oh..." Serena blushed, "Right."

As the control center came to life, Zane began toggling switches and typing commands. Taking this in for as long as she could manage, Serena soon became bored and turned away from him to explore the room.

"Wouldn't have killed the old man to put a little color in this place," she sneered, taking in the solid-white walls and ceiling—still illuminated by the just-as-white fluorescent lights—and a floor that seemed to be made of a single piece of cold, lifeless rock that reflected the light above it along its dull-gray surface.

"I think you're missing the point of why this is here," Zane sighed as a final keystroke was applied and the whirring of activity began.

Startled by the noise, Serena whimpered as the lights dimmed to nearly nothing before flashing brighter than before and leveling out once again. "Wh-what the—"

Zane took her quaking shoulders into his palms to steady her nerves, "It's fine, princess! That was just the power shifting to the other generators. Everything should be up and running now."

She blushed, biting her lip at both her reaction and Zane's touch and she nodded, shrugging free of his hands. "Does this place have running water? I'd like to take a shower."

Zane frowned and nodded, "Yea. We used preexisting sewer systems to avoid the hassle of putting in new plumbing and tapped a public water main that runs beneath the park. The boiler still needs to heat up, so it might be a little bit before we have hot water."

"At this point I don't care," Serena laughed, "Just as long as I *know* that I'll be able to wash this ash out of my hair!"

Though she shouldn't have been surprised by the outcome of the group's pairing, she was nevertheless taken back when she discovered she'd be sharing a room with Zane. Even more alarming was the realization that she wasn't opposed to the situation.

As it turned out, a "limited" number of rooms turned out to be a dozen—the hall that Zoey had led the group down earlier forking off into two others which had six rooms sectioned each—and this meant that, between the group of 26 vampires and therions, every room was occupied by two—and in two of the more "fortunate" rooms, three—irritated Mythos.

Serena scoffed and shook her head as she rinsed the shampoo from her hair for the fourth time. Given all the facts, she found herself playfully calculating how long it would be before a fight broke out between their haphazard group.

Except for Isaac and Zoey, of course, who had all but leapt at the chance to share a room. While Serena was *sure* they were at each other's throats, she was *also* sure that neither of them minded.

Chuckling at the sheer calamity of the whole mess, she grabbed the shampoo bottle to begin her fifth lathering. A dime-sized bead of the viscous, amber fluid landed in her palm before it choked out its last drop and made an obscene noise. "Fuck!" She sighed. No matter how many times she scrubbed and rinsed she felt hidden under a film of soot and grime. Giving her body one final rinse before deciding that nothing short of a fire hose would do the job; she turned off the water and stepped out of the shower.

At least she had a room attached to a private bathroom.

She rolled her eyes; the perks of bunking with her father's favorite warrior.

The towels, like the bathroom—like the halls and like every square-goddam-foot of their underground safe-haven—were white. Cursing at the bleached prison, she violently snatched one of them up and began to dry; doing everything in her power to sully the immaculate cloth's surface and failing miserably.

Perhaps Keith wouldn't have to kill her, after all, since she would probably have a seizure when she was once again introduced to *any* color that was rapidly becoming a distant memory in her mind.

She smirked at the idea of ripping Zane's throat open and putting a little red on the walls.

And then regretted it just as fast as she'd humored it.

What the hell was happening to her?

Slipping into a pair of sweat pants and a tank-top that Zane had given her, she tied back her hair and stepped out into the room.

Crossing the threshold, she shivered at the change in temperature and took a moment to adjust as she looked over to find Zane hunched over a desk in the corner of the room. Though everything—every-goddam-thing—was evenly lit by the all-seeing fluorescents, something in his features seemed shadowed and, as a result, aggressive. His gaze, locked between his palms, which lay flat on the table's surface and shivered intermittently, seemed to be wilder and less focused than usual.

"Zane?" her voice came out as a whisper, though she hadn't intended it to. He whipped his head towards her; his mismatched eyes flashing with the intensity and rage that she'd come to expect from his beast-state. She frowned and forced herself to take a step towards him. Even with all his strength and all the danger he wielded, she couldn't bring herself to blame him for any of it. She knew he was tortured; tormented by whatever it was those tattoos were put on him for. "It's okay. It's going to be alright." She walked over towards him; her bare arms tingling as her flesh tightened and left goose-bumps. Slowly, trying not to startle him, she placed her left hand on his shoulder and began to absorb some of his excess energy in an attempt to calm him.

Feeling the sudden drain, Zane's eyes became tired and half-lidded as his body and aura started to lose their tension. She could tell he was trying to relax—could see enough into his mind to watch him regain enough focus to begin counteracting the effects of his rage—and he began clenching and unclenching his fists repeatedly. When he reopened his eyes, they were a dimmer gold, looking suddenly tired and worn-out, and looked up at her face.

"S-sorry..." Sis speech was slurred from exhaustion.

Serena shook her head and slowly pulled her hand away, "Don't be. I know it's not your—"

"But it *is*! It's anger! *My* anger. Mine! Not the damn curse's; *MINE!*" His body tensed and went rigid as his aura flared and he snarled from the second wave of anger. Serena started to reach for him but he shook his head, forcing his eyes shut and inhaling sharply and continuing to clench and unclench his fists until he'd relaxed again; this time seeming even more drained from the process. "Th-they saw it; saw the *real* me and used it as a trigger. They booby-trapped my own anger to cause this..." He spoke, his voice coming out more of a growl and he forced an exhale and shook his head, "I couldn't control it to begin with. But now... *now* the damn thing *knows*. It sees a way out and it's doing all it can to do just that," he looked up at her, his eyes sad and pleading. "I... I can actually *feel* it in my head, lurking about and trying to find the right triggers to push me over the edge. And... and I'm starting to want it; I actually *want* to let it out... but I don't know if those are my thoughts or its. And I can't help but wonder, wh-who the fuck am I anymore?"

She frowned and leaned over to him. She wanted to help him, to make him feel at peace just as much as she did with him. "It's okay. I'm here for you, Zane, and I still know who you are," she said softly, offering him a smile, "Who you *really* are."

Zane frowned, shaking his head, "Why should you care?"

Serena bit her lip, kneeling down, "Because I *do*!"

"Hardly!" he scoffed, "I *heard* you and your ghost—your lover, right?—talking about me!" He shook his head as his long, unkempt dark hair shook more in his face. "We're not right, right? That's what you said! What you told *him*!" He forced himself to relax again and groaned as his head rolled about on his shoulders, "Don't pretend to care about me just to make me feel better. It'll only piss me off more."

She frowned, freezing her grip as she watched the emotions cave into his face as he confessed hearing Devon and her conversation. And while she remembered *saying* the words, she couldn't recall if she'd ever *believed* them. She bit her lip. Was she falling for Zane? Could she *actually* get over Devon, even with him still *haunting* her? She had sworn to be faithful—had even been ready to *marry* Devon—but what did that mean now? Looking into Zane's golden eyes, she suddenly felt like everything was right. There was no more doubt or panic at not knowing what was coming, because she at least knew that he wouldn't let her face it alone.

And she found herself forgetting...

She nodded, "I... I *did* say that, but I—"

No! Stop it, Serena! Devon pulled away from her, using her aura to build his mock-body as he always had before; hollow and translucent and trapped in her aura because neither of them was ready to let go of the other. She couldn't even remember what it was like to *not* have him attached to her auric field. And now he was pulling at her; using more energy than he ever had before in an effort to pull her away from Zane. *You're mine!* **Mine!** His voice bellowed in her head and the dresser on the other side of the room began to shake.

She cried out, gripping her head and dropping to her knees as Devon howled and pulled at her, "N-no! Devon... please! I can't... I can't keep... don't make me..."

Zane's eyes flashed again and a deep growl emitted from his throat as his aura began to shift from blue-to-red, his eyes widening momentarily before narrowing in on Devon.

He could *see* him?

"Get away from her! Leave her alone, you clingy bastard! Can't you see you're *hurting* her?" Zane yelled.

Devon whipped and writhed in rage at the accusation and

Zane's hair shifted from the force, *We were fine until you showed up, monster! We were together and we were happy and—*

"Happy? Sitting alone in some shit-hole in the woods with nobody but a *ghost* to keep her company? And a *pussy* of a ghost, at that! You think she was *happy* like that?"

"Zane...Devon..." Serena whimpered and turned to Devon, growing more uncertain.

No! I won't let it end like this! I'm doing what I should have done in the beginning! Devon flew at Zane, beginning to tear free of Serena's purple aura and disappearing for a moment before emerging once again in Zane's; her ghostly lover now bathed in scarlet as he struggled to take control of Zane's body.

Zane growled, fighting back Devon's advances as he steadily lost more and more of himself to the invasion. As Zane's life began to drain from his eyes and Devon's force began to occupy them, the body began to shake with violent spasms.

"Devon! Get out of him now! This isn't the right way to do it!" Serena cried out, taking Zane's shoulders and shaking him.

"Too late," Zane's eyes shifted and glassed over as Devon took control. As Serena watched, the last auric tendril receded back into the body as he finished.

"Z-Zane?" Serena frowned, stepping back, "I didn't... where? Where is he? Where is his aura?" she began to shake, feeling cold and alone and, worst of all, whole. The part of her aura that Devon had occupied for all those years had been returned to her, and the new sense of strength was overwhelming.

"Serena!" Zane's voice seemed different with Devon using it, "I did it! I got him!" He looked at his new hands and examined his face, beginning to laugh excitedly as he confirmed his success, "I'm... I'm back! I have a—"

"How could you do this?" she screamed at him, "You knew this wasn't the way! You knew this was wrong! It wasn't supposed to be like this!"

Devon stepped towards her, his motions clunky and uncoordinated in his new body, "Don't you see? Now you don't have to *choose* between him and me! You can have *me* in *his* body!" He smiled, but it looked foreign and wrong on Zane's face, "It can be like we always wanted!"

"I never wanted this! You've... you've *killed* him! I can't even *see* a trace of him left! We were never supposed to *steal* a body, Devon!" She sobbed, shaking her head.

He frowned and stared in disbelief, "Were you... did you actually *feel* something for him? Something past just this body? I thought—"

"You thought wrong!" She hissed, glaring at him through tear-filled eyes. "You've been dead too long, Devon! You aren't like you were! You *never* would've done this before! You might be Devon's aura... but you're not him! Not anymore!"

He sneered, shaking his head angrily, "You... you're lying! You betrayed me! You said 'forever'! You promised..." He flinched and looked down at his arm as the tattoos began to glow, "What? What is this? Who are—" he shook and dropped to his knees, whimpering as his aura began to inflate and shine brighter than before; the red becoming so massive and overwhelming that the entire room looked like it was bathed in blood. His body continued to shake at the aura's epicenter as swirls of new color—new aura—began to writhe through the calamity. "H-HOW ARE YOU..." He clutched his head and whimpered before twitching violently and snarling. "You're not welcome in me either, you phantom fuck!" The body lurched forward with a tremor as its joints began to break and shift with the start of the transformation and the bright, pained eyes locked on Serena as Zane's voice—Zane's *real* voice— came through:

"Get out! Go get Zoey and wait for meeEEEAAAHHHHHHHH!"

Serena tried to run to him but was overpowered by his aura and thrown towards the door. Crying at the impact, she pulled herself up, giving one last glimpse at the chaos before she rushed out the door and into the hallway.

Zoey!

Had to find Zoey!

She frowned, trying to remember the right path as she began to maneuver through the ghostly-white catacombs.

It wasn't until she saw Zoey running towards her that she realized she'd been calling her name.

"Serena! What is it? What's wrong?"

"Zoey! It's Zane! I think he's…" She choked on the words and lost her voice as she buried her face into Zoey's shoulder.

CHAPTER TEN
MONSTERS

ZANE COULDN'T FORGIVE HIMSELF. He had become the monster plenty of times before—more times than he dared to imagine—and it had always ended in disaster.

Although it wasn't new...

...it had never been this personal.

And while he had struggled in the past to keep at least a part of himself in control—enough to not destroy *everything!*—he had succumbed entirely to its wishes this time.

The memory of Serena as she hit the door flashed in his mind.

The look of pain and confusion and terror in her eyes right

before she'd left the room in a panic.

She'd trusted him! She'd cared about him! She was the only person left who didn't see him as an unstable weapon ready to explode at any moment. And he'd hurt her...

He'd given her reason to fear him.

He had hurt not only the woman he cared for, but, in doing so, he had destroyed the ghost—the one she truly loved—in a jealous rage.

No. Not destroyed...

Eradicated!

It was no accident; no fault of the curse or its influences.

He'd *wanted* it!

Needed to destroy what stood in his way.

He shook his head as he thought of the rage as he'd reacquired his body from Serena's lover. In his fury—in his *need* to be rid of him—he'd dismantled every fiber of Devon's aura.

And he'd made sure it hurt.

Zane groaned and splashed more water on his face. He hadn't even *known* such a thing was possible...

But apparently the beast did.

It showed him *exactly* how to destroy every last trace of his competition until he was certain there'd be nothing left to send to wherever it was they went to.

And he'd *loved* it!

He truly was a monster.

He looked in the mirror and saw that his eyes, though still bloodshot, had finally shifted back to their normal shade.

"You will live with the guilt of your true self until the day the beast consumes it all. You will perish knowing that, even in death, you will only cause more suffering."

The rasping voice of the Taroe elder and his explanation of the curse the night he'd been given the tattoos echoed in his head. He let himself remember the pain he endured that night; the burning of the mystical ink as it was stabbed and scraped across his chest and back and arms while the Taroe tribe chanted in celebration of his punishment.

Maybe it would be best if he left. Maybe he could find a place where he couldn't harm another; where the beast could destroy him and no more harm would have to fall on anyone else.

Maybe, in torturing himself, he could spare the world.

"Maybe I should just go home," Serena grumbled into the palms of her hands as Zoey did her best to soothe her.

"He's really become *that* overcome by that curse then?" Isaac asked, looking at Zoey with a deepening frown.

Zoey sighed and nodded, leaning her forehead against his stomach as he stepped over to the two.

Serena bit her lip as she watched Zoey and Isaac's interactions. Even in a moment of seriousness their body language spoke wonders. Though they'd only been together a short period of time, they seemed so happy already. So perfect!

She scowled and looked away, holding back her envy.

"He was so angry! Even his eyes looked different!" She explained, "He kept trying to relax, but it just kept coming back!"

Zoey nodded slowly, "His rage is beginning to overwhelm him..."

Serena looked up, "He said that..." She frowned, trying to recall, "... that the curse wasn't the cause of his rage. Is that right?"

"We can't be certain of that," Zoey shrugged, "None of us knew him before it happened. Gregori took him in after he found him trying to drink himself to death."

"But vampires can't get drunk..." Serena frowned and looked up.

Zoey nodded, sighing, "Yup. And *that* only served to fuel his rage further. So Gregori decided, since both you and your brother had left, that he could take Zane in and try to turn his life around." She gave a gentle smirk, "To try to give him a fresh start on a new path."

"Did it work?" Serena asked.

"More or less, I suppose," Zoey shrugged one shoulder, "Zane certainly took to the training well, and it wasn't long after that he began climbing the ranks as a clan warrior. That had *seemed* to turn things around, but as his fits of rage became rarer and rarer the curse became that much more sensitive to the slightest trigger." She scoffed at a memory and shook her head, "He *destroyed* his first room—and this was a *nice* room, mind you; Gregori pampered him well—when he stubbed his toe on a door frame one night. By the time we'd gotten him sedated he'd already torn down the wall surrounding that door and most of the walls surrounding it for good measure. Gregori had scolded him later over how costly his temper was becoming."

Serena frowned and looked down, remembering how Zane had lectured her about the cost of maintaining the clan. "So is his rage a side-effect of the curse, or is the curse piggy-backing on what was already there?"

Zoey frowned, "I'm certain that he had anger problems long before the Taroe put the curse on him—I'm guessing they saw it as a cruel irony to make his short fuse a *literal* one—but I also think that knowing what his rage was capable of after that made it that much harder to control."

Isaac frowned, "Like when you *know* you shouldn't think of something...?"

"Then that's *all* you can think about," Zoey nodded, "The curse has been eating away at him ever since, and every transformation has been just one more step towards having that thing take over him completely. That seems to be the bulk of the curse, to slowly destroy the victim from the inside by turning their worst trait against them." She rubbed her forehead and winced, "If he's so far gone—if the rage has consumed him *that* much—it may already be too late."

"What do you mean? What will happen to him?" Serena asked, panicking.

"The Taroe are tribes of magic practicing humans that have

separated themselves from society. They live peaceful and self-contained lives and have, over time, developed a method of focusing one's magical energies through an enchanted ink that they use to tattoo themselves. When one of them comes of age they're given their first tattoo, and with every following year or every shift in the tribe's rank more tattoos are added. Usually, the ink serves to channel the wearer's thoughts to boost their power, but there's something different in Zane's case. The ink triggers from his rage and the magic starts the transformation, but his body wasn't made for that sort of thing. While Isaac and other therions are naturally built to shift forms, Zane's isn't; so every transformation takes a greater and greater toll on him."

Serena looked up at Zoey and shook her head, getting more and more irritated by the idea of somebody *willingly* doing this to Zane, "But what does Zane have to do with the Taroe? Since when do they get involved with our kind?"

Zoey shrugged, "Normally they never would. Most can't even say they've found a Taroe tribe, much less been cursed by one. But while he *was* just a sang—and not even pure-born, at that—the curse has altered him. Though he shouldn't be able to see or use any of his auric channels, he's achieved auric feats in his beast form that most need years of training to accomplish. He can see in multiple spectrums; going beyond simple vision or seeing auras, but heat radiation, ultraviolet, gamma…" She shook her head, "When he becomes that thing there seems to be no limit. I watched him change in the middle of a fight against a gang of rogues, and in the middle of the chaos one of them took a sword to his leg! Cut it clean off from the knee!" She sighed, "And the damn thing just grew a new one right there. Then it made a note of using what the vampire had cut off to beat him to death. If it wants something badly enough, it adapts to find a way."

"Oh my god…" Serena stared in shock at her friend, "B-but… why? Why give him that kind of strength?"

"Because strength without control is crippling," Zoey sighed. "He can't trust himself in a fight, because the moment *it* comes out there's no control over who it kills. He's already been seen as too much of a risk with other warriors from the clan who wouldn't get within five meters of him! The power isn't the curse, Serena, the curse is not being able to contain or direct it and having to live with the knowledge of what it's done and the lives it's ruined.

"In the end—when he turns back; when he becomes *Zane* once again—he's no more powerful than he would have been before the curse. No auric control or enhanced vampire strengths. Just another sang that has to own up to something no sang should ever be capable of doing."

"So the Taroes were willing to put so many lives at risk just to make Zane feel *guilty*?" Serena growled.

Zoey sighed and nodded, "It would certainly seem that way. I can't vouch for either of them; I wasn't there. I hadn't even *heard* of something like this before, so I have to imagine it doesn't happen too often. Whatever their intentions were, it worked, his mind's beginning to break from the guilt and the torment on his body, and the only thing that seems to slow down the process is you."

Serena's eyes widened and she looked over, "Me? You mean that he's never..." She frowned, "Why me? He didn't even *know* me until the other night!"

"Either way," Zoey stood up and stepped beside Isaac, "you seem to have some sway over it; something that *nobody* else has, and that makes you vital to our survival and his."

"What the hell am I supposed to do? I don't think he'll even *want* to talk to me after what just happened, and I don't know how I'm supposed to face him knowing what he did to..." Serena frowned and looked down, still upset about the loss of Devon. Though she couldn't put all the blame on Zane for what had happened, it was easier than the alternative.

"I can't tell you what to do, Serena. You'll need to decide that. I just hope you can come to understand that he's not a monster. He's gotten that for far too long already," Zoey took Isaac's hand and she offered Serena a comforting though forced smile before they left to head back to their room.

120

"Right… Thanks, Zoey."

Serena sighed, thinking back to her memories with Devon and how he had always been there for her. She sighed and gazed down at the ring she still wore.

Rolling it on her finger, she felt a lump form in her throat as her body shook from the flood of memories; memories that she didn't want—didn't *need*—to remember anymore. She'd been using those memories and the biased emotions they carried as a crutch for too long in the past. Now, she had to look at the reality of it all.

Devon was gone now.

Completely.

So what would he have wanted her to do?

She frowned at the question.

What would he *really* have wanted her to do?

In his final moments he had been so aggressive and uncontrollable—so *not* himself—in his struggle to get control of Zane's body… and she'd fought him. Why? Just a few days ago she would've looked the other way and let Devon have *any* body he'd wanted—dead *or* alive—just so she could have him touch her again. But when it was Zane's body he was after—Zane's *mind* at risk—she had tried to stop him. Serena groaned and cupped her face in her hands again as she struggled with the realization that she wasn't just in love with Zane's body—hell, she'd been seconds away from having *that* all she wanted!—but that, for him in his entirety, she was willing to let Devon go.

Literally!

Years upon years of love and adoration and promise and effort put against several days of insults and banter and teasing and mocking.

And she'd chosen the latter…

She shook her head and cursed at herself.

When had she allowed herself to become a monster?

CHAPTER ELEVEN
PAIN

ZANE CRIED OUT AS HE FIRED another round from the Beretta into his thigh and, feeling the burning of the beast threatening to break free, slammed the barrel against his temple and tensed his finger around the trigger.

"Give me a reason, you son of a bitch! You take one goddam step into the open and I'm blowing our fucking brains out! Do you hear me, motherfucker?"

The burning subsided and the tattoos faded back to black.

"Yea. Thought so! Let's see how long you can keep it up!" Zane scoffed, moving the barrel back to his thigh and firing another shot; crying out once again at the jolt of pain that struck his thigh.

Just then the door flew open, now wearing a foot-shaped crater where it had been kicked.

Serena glared in at him, taking in the scene and scowling more. "You idiot!" Serena growled as she stomped into the room, slamming the door shut behind her and latching it with her aura. Zane tightened his grip on the gun, bracing for her to try to pull it from him, only to have her yank it from him with her aura. "You fucking *idiot!*" As she closed the distance between them, she drew back her fist and punched him straight in the jaw, sending him sailing off the bed and straight into the wall. She stared down at her hand for a moment, surprised at her own strength.

Surprised, but not regretful.

Not in the least!

She narrowed her eyes and rushed at him again, putting another fist into his stomach.

He wretched and whimpered.

She glared down at him and reveled in the bittersweet irony that losing Devon had actually made her stronger!

He groaned and lifted his mismatched blue and silver eyes to her. "Serena…" He croaked, still in obvious pain from her attack.

"You bastard! What the fuck were you doing? Trying to *lure* it out so you could have an excuse to *kill* yourself?" She shook her head and spat at his feet, "You're a fool! A goddam *idiot!* We need you right now! The clan needs you! God-fucking-dammit, Zane, *I* need you!"

He looked down and frowned, the shame of Devon's death still twisted on his face.

She rolled her eyes and sighed, slumping down beside him. She couldn't hate him; not even if she wanted to.

"I'm sorry, Serena. I really am," he covered his face with his hands to hide his paint-filled eyes. "I—fuck!—I don't even know what to say to make it better; I don't even know if I *could* make it better. It's never been like…" He sighed and started to chuckle,

"I'm usually not *this* fucked up." His laughs had no trace of mirth in them.

"Zane... what happened to Devon?" Serena frowned, looking over at him.

"Do you want me to answer that truthfully?" He shifted his gaze to meet hers, "Because, truthfully, I can't say for certain. I don't know where he is now. Fuck, I don't even know if he's *anywhere*; I didn't think you could *destroy* energy—I mean, a goddam middle school teacher can tell you it's impossible—but I'll be damned if it"—he shook his head and corrected himself—"if *I* didn't find a way! I just couldn't control it any longer... I *wanted* to kill him; I wanted to get rid of him so you and I could..." He lifted his bloodshot eyes to hers suddenly before glancing down at her lips.

Realizing what he was staring at, she instinctively moved to wet her lips, but caught herself in time to avoid a lewd display. She shook her head at her own reaction and looked away.

"Zane..." Her mind was even more conflicted now. He was jealous of Devon! He had wanted her for himself and he'd killed Devon—a dead man—to get to her.

And she couldn't bring herself to resent him for it.

And then it hit her...

She was attracted to Zane more than she ever could have thought possible. She bit her lip, trying to think of when her feelings had really started. That time they were training she felt the attraction more than she cared to admit. Still, she needed to see if her attraction was genuine.

She needed to see how far it went.

Lifting her head, she took his face in her hands and brought him to meet her gaze before she leaned in to kiss him, only to have her advance halted by his hand. Her eyes widened, startled at his intervention and she bit her lip as she saw that he was glaring at her.

A moment of silence passed, and as she studied his face she realized he wasn't looking *at* her, but *past* her. He was staring at the door!

In a flash he was on his feet and planting himself between her and the door as a blood-red aura passed through and unlocked it from the other side, allowing it to swing open on the warped hinges from Serena's assault on it.

"Am I intruding?" Keith smirked, leaning casually against the doorframe and eating an apple.

"How did you get in here?" Zane glared, feeling his anger rising once again. Though he was eager to give in to it—to let the beast break free and do what it did best and finally be done with Keith and his bullshit—he couldn't bring himself to relinquish his control. He had no way of insuring that, if released, it would stop there, and with Serena in the room he couldn't risk a total loss of control. He scowled, but nevertheless forced himself to take a deep breath and suppress the urge to free it.

"Ah! I see you're learning to control it, eh? Pity. Seems like it could be useful, doesn't it?" Keith scoffed, taking another bite from the apple and shaking his head, "A *fun* punishment. Sort of defeats the purpose if you ask me," he grinned and looked over at Serena, "I'm sorry, sis, am I interrupting something? I wouldn't have pegged you as the sort, but this doesn't seem too far from *bestiality*, wouldn't you say? First a human and now this," he clucked his tongue, "What would our parents think?"

"Shut up, you son of a bitch! Our parents are *dead* because of you, so I'm sure they'd have rather seen me hook on a fucking street corner before approving of your decisions!" She shot to her feet and glared, stepping beside Zane, "This is all your fault! Everything that's happened—from the very beginning—has been entirely your fault! You killed Mom and blamed it on our father to turn me against him! You've manipulated me every step of the way to trick me into believing you!"

Keith shrugged and let the apple fall from his palm and roll across the floor as he took a step inside, "What can I say? I've always been something of a trouble-maker, right? Bit of a problem-child?" He sneered at them, casually glancing about the room despite their defensive stances against him, "I'm sure your new boyfriend has said it all; parroting all the same bullshit Daddy dearest crammed into his mind. An exaggeration on an exaggeration on an exaggeration... oh yes, you should most certainly believe *that* sort of credibility! Leave now, Serena. The door is right there and I won't do anything to stop you. My business is and always has been with your beasty boy-toy." He glared at her, "But your safety relies on your abandonment of the Clan of Vail, so if you intend on rejoining them, you're accepting their fate!"

"Do as he says, Serena! This doesn't need to be your fight! Get out of here!" Zane growled, shaking as he said the words but never once relinquishing his death-glare on Keith.

"No fucking way am I le—"

Zane grabbed her before she could finish and shoved her towards the door, "I said get out NOW!" He fought the growing rage, holding back its efforts to take control long enough to herd Serena out, "Go! Find Zoey and Isaac; *everybody*! Tell them to get out of here—to abandon Vail and everything to do with it—and make new lives elsewhere!" Zane gave her another shove towards the door.

He watched as she stumbled through the door and turned to come back again, "No! I won't leave you!"

Zane shot her a glare, his aura already shifting red and giving him the ability to slam the door in her face, lock it, and barricade it against her enraged shrieks and brutal assault to try to get through. Keith smirked at the racket and arched an eyebrow at Zane as her futile efforts resounded within the room.

"Zane! Goddam it!" She screamed through the door, "Let me in!"

Keith chuckled, "Tenacious little bitch, isn't she?"

Zane continued to glare at him, not offering a response.

"Ah yes, straight to business, right? My father *has* taught you well. Alright then, if that's how it must be..." Keith inhaled sharply as his aura extended from each wrist and his hands began to glow as he wrapped each fist in it.

Zane glared and pulled his Beretta into his hand with his own aura and took aim at Keith's head. "I should warn you: though it's the beast that you've come to recognize me for, I *was* recognized by your father and many others as a capable warrior on my own. Allow me to demonstrate my marksmanship."

"Not fighting fair, I see," Keith glared.

"I'm willing to bet you wouldn't either," Zane spat, letting the burning of his tattoos envelop his arms as he guided his aura towards the Beretta, "Now let's see if there's any merit to your sister's methods!" as he spoke, one of his auric tendrils covered the gun and wrapped around the round already waiting in the chamber as he pulled the trigger. Keith glared and moved to dodge the shot, but Zane, anticipating this, redirected the bullet in his aura and drove it into Keith's shoulder. Hissing in pain, Keith glared down at the wound and gaped at the sight of Zane's auric tendril still clinging to the burning metal inside him. Zane smirked, extending another auric tendril to the next waiting round. "Oh yes! Definitely on to something here!"

He twisted the slug within the meat of Keith's muscle, causing his shoulder to spasm violently as he hissed in pain.

"AH!" he gritted his teeth and glared at Zane, "So, you *are* learning to control it?" Keith growled and, focusing past the pain in his shoulder, charged at him in overdrive.

Zane frowned, caught off guard by Keith's swiftness, and cried out as he was thrown against the wall. Appearing in front of him a moment later, Keith grabbed him by the throat and drove his aura into his chest, pushing him harder into the wall, twisting and crumpling its surface as he did.

As Zane's aura shriveled with a loss of focus, his hold on the slug in Keith's shoulder slipped, allowing Keith to pull it out with his own aura and let it drop to the floor.

"Now *that* was rude!" he hissed, extending his fangs as he drove more pressure into his assault on Zane's body.

As the last of his breath was forced from his lungs, Zane gasped and struggled to keep his focus against Keith's efforts to crush him.

He couldn't let him win!

Not now!

"You knew this was coming, beast! You've been waiting *years* for it, right? Waiting for the day you wouldn't have to suffer and grieve and *feel?*" He smirked and began to drain Zane's aura with his own, taking away the rage and stifling any hope of transforming, and chuckling as his eyes began to lose focus.

Zane gargled on his words; both his intended message and its delivery a mystery to both of them as his mind grew too hazy to think. Keith began to laugh—the sound echoing and rolling irregularly in Zane's ears—and, taking Zane's gun from his flaccid grip, brought it to his stomach.

"I can't kill you just yet; not if I hope to achieve what I've worked so hard towards. But, in case you doubt my sincerity in this issue, here's a little souvenir." He wrapped his own aura around the gun as Zane had and pulled back the trigger, sending the aura-laced bullet into Zane's guts, twisting and stirring it about as emphasis. Zane whimpered and shook as Keith released his hold and allowed him to fall to the floor, smirking as he began to heave and cough up blood. "Yes, it *is* quite painful, isn't it? I thought it was unfair to savor all of *that* on my own," he laughed and stood up, leering down at him. "I hope I've made my point, Zane," he poked the toe of his shoe into the gunshot wound and smirked at the pained grunt, "It's better if you stay out of my way."

With his auric barricade receding, Serena's ongoing assault on the door finally paid off and the door flew open on shrieking hinges.

"Keith! You bastard!" She shot forward and released a wave of auric arrows at her brother.

But he was already in overdrive and gone from the room and

the safe house—leaving behind the lingering echoes of his laughter—by the time they found purchase against the far wall.

As she withdrew her aura back into herself and hurried to Zane, his vision faded and the world went black.

Zoey sighed, "He'll live through this, though we're lucky he didn't transform."

"It was Keith… the bastard had nearly drained him to the point of death!" Serena bit her lip, looking down at Zane's unconscious body, "There was nothing to fuel the change!"

"I hate to say it, but he may owe Keith his life."

Serena glared at Zoey, "Are you serious? *Look* what that fuck did to him!"

"But it *could* have been worse!" Zoey sighed, wrapping the last of Zane's bandages as an I.V. of enchanted synth-blood fed into his vein.

"What will we do next time if Keith appears again? What *can* we do?" Serena growled, "He's too fucking strong! The next time he might not stop at just *mutilating* us! Can't we just *give* him whatever it is he's after?" Serena growled, "He'll have no reason to hurt us if we're not standing in his way!"

"It's not that simple, Serena. Keith's been playing with those at The Council; feeding them lies and using the influence they've given him so that he can acquire Vail and dismantle it from the inside."

"Okay? So my brother's a bitter, power-hungry, spoiled little bitch-boy!" Serena sneered, "Tell me something I don't know, like *why* we have to suffer any longer to protect a clan that's *already* destroyed from being taken by a prick aiming to *destroy* it?"

"Because his efforts have labeled us as the bad guys to The Council, and *that* means we're bad guys to *everyone* that serves them!" Zoey sighed, "But they're organized. They have rules and regulations on how to approach these situations. *That's* why Zane's still alive! If Keith kills him now, he's breaking protocol. If we hand Keith the clan, we hand him the *only* thing that's keeping The Council from executing us on the spot!

"If we lose the title that Vail gives us—what it represents to The Council's codes—then we'll be deemed rogues and we'll all be killed!"

"But there *is* no Clan of Vail anymore! How are we under its protection?"

"Because it's *politics*, Serena! Until all the right steps are taken—all the paperwork filed and all the proper authorities notified and consenting—to *classify* Vail as a dead clan, then neither they *nor* Keith can act on it!"

Serena looked down at Zane, "So if Keith kills Zane before then…"

Zoey nodded, "Then *he* will be executed for breaking The Council's protocol and killing a clan warrior without due cause."

Serena sighed, "And killing Keith would give them due cause, wouldn't it?"

"I'm afraid so."

"So—what?—we're dead if we hold on to the title of Vail and we're dead if we hand it over, is that right?" Serena snarled.

"Pretty much…" Zoey nodded.

Isaac thought for a moment, "But what if we can get to The Council and *show* them what a manipulative little shit Keith is? Obviously *we* have no authority, but I'm sure they'd be *pissed* if they saw how he's been screwing with their system, right?"

Zoey smirked, "Oh, I can't even *imagine* what sort of punishment they'd have lined up for *that* sort of an offense. Though they *do* love to make examples out of the more severe—"

"No! I *will* kill my brother for everything he's done!" Serena snarled. "I don't care if The Council executes me for it! It's better that our bloodline dies with me avenging my parents!"

Zoey glared, "And what about *our* lives, Serena? What about *Zane's* life? If you kill Keith, you validate every claim he's made against us and we'll all be killed!" She sighed, seeing the pain in

Serena's eyes as this fact dawned upon her and she offered a reassuring smile, "Look, The Council *will* deal with him when they see what he's done. I promise. What they will do to him will make death seem like an act of mercy. If there's anything The Council loathes over anything else, it's anything that might motivate an uprising against them, and a corrupt influence in their ranks is a *severe* threat to their authority over the Mythos community."

Serena frowned and nodded, hoping that what Zoey said wasn't just an empty promise to make her feel better. Looking down at Zane, she watched as his wound began to heal and let out a relieved breath.

"We need to be more careful from now on," Serena frowned.

"Agreed," Zoey nodded.

Isaac smirked and nodded as well, gesturing towards some of his pack mates that stood with the remaining Vail warriors, "And you'll have plenty of help, too."

Zoey frowned, "You know you don't have to help us, Isaac. You and your pack aren't a part of this."

"Like hell we aren't!" Isaac growled, "That bastard's vendetta dragged my pack into this shitstorm! He's gotten our brothers and sisters *killed* so that he could exact some petty revenge in response to a family feud! Oh you bet your ass we are a part of this!"

Zane let out a small groan and his body was beginning to shiver as his wounds continued to knit closed. His mismatched eyes shot open then and he cried out as his tattoos began to glow.

"H-hot!" he groaned.

"He should be healing faster than this," Zoey frowned, chewing at her lip.

"It's okay, Zoey. I think I might be able to help him this time," Serena smiled at them and nodded.

Zoey blinked for a moment, caught off guard by the response, but finally smiled and nodded. "Sounds good. We'll go get some towels and ice," she motioned for Isaac and the others to follow her.

When they were alone, Serena looked down at Zane, laying a

hand on his sweat-covered forehead, "It'll be ok," she whispered as she pulled several strands of his hair from his face, "I'm not going anywhere."

Before long Zoey returned with several clean towels and a bucket of ice and they began to work on relieving Zane of his burning skin. As the cool cloth touched his forehead, he let out a startled gasp and began to shiver; the glow of his tattoos starting to dim. Serena smiled at the progress and continued, leaning down to examine his wound and discovering that the synth-blood had run its course and healed him.

"Serena…" Zane smiled as his eyes focused on her.

Serena couldn't help but smile as she found herself staring back into his eyes.

Zoey, seeing that she was no longer needed, made a quick-but-silent exit to leave them alone.

Overwhelmed by her emotions, Serena leaned back in the chair that she'd pulled up next to Zane's bed earlier.

"I'm glad you're ok now," she whispered.

"Yea. All thanks to your stubbornness!" Zane sighed, "You shouldn't have stayed!" Though he fought to keep his eyes away, she could see he didn't believe what he was saying.

"Fuck that! I wasn't about to let you have all the fun!" She smirked at his resulting sneer, "I'm going to help one way or another! After all, he *is* my brother and Vail *is* my clan!"

"So you're *not* going to kill him?" Zane gave her a skeptical stare, "Be honest."

She sighed and nodded, "Yea, I guess if The Council can do better than I can it's worth it to let them do their job."

Zane smirked, "It *will* be impressive."

"And I should stick around to keep you from going Hulk and spoiling it all! Guess we're lucky your curse-beast has a hard-on for me," she smirked.

Zane blushed and bit his lip, sitting up. "You know… he's not the only one." He frowned and shook his head, "Not that that's the only thing I care abo—"

"It's okay, I understand. I just... I need a little more time to get over Devon," she bit her lip and turned away, feeling the tears starting to well in her eyes. "I hope you understand."

There was no response.

Frowning at the silence, Serena turned back, realizing that Zane was gone..

CHAPTER TWELVE
REVELATIONS

"SERENA! WE NEED TO DO something! We can't wait for Zane anymore!"

"How far are we going to make it without him, Zoey?" Serena glared, "I won't reconsider this! We *have* to find him!"

"If we waste any more time it might be too late for *any* of us," Isaac growled, slamming his fist into the walls, "He knows where we are and how to get in, and we can't just keep sleeping in shifts and hoping we're not attacked again! Waiting on him isn't an option!"

"It is for me!" Serena growled at both of them, "He left *because* of me! I can't just—"

"Will you stop being so goddam selfish just because you've suddenly realized and admitted your feelings for him? We can't wait anymore! We have precious little time and far too many things to do in that time!" Zoey cried out, tears growing in her eyes, "I *know* Zane! I've known him far longer than you've known him and I can tell you with all certainty that, wherever he is, he's doing something *stupid*. And with Zane, stupid gets people *killed!*"

Serena frowned and froze at the words. Her mind had been wracked for the last few days and she had locked herself away from the others and delaying every attempt to leave, hoping that Zane would come back. But there still had been no sign of him. In that time, however, she had come to terms over Devon's "death" and decided that mourning wasn't doing her any good; especially since she'd been mourning his death for *years* now. Just because a shadow of his personality had lingered and clung to her didn't mean that she had to waste her life trying to find a way to reverse the irreversible. No matter what they would've done—no matter what sort of body they could've obtained for him—it still wouldn't have changed that he *was* dead and that she should've let him go—figuratively *and* literally—all those years ago.

Mourning and regret and doing nothing were something she had gotten very good at, and in all that time she'd been miserable and alone and achieved nothing.

It was time to stop waiting and hoping the world would fix itself around her.

It was time to take action.

She looked over at the others and nodded. "You're right," she sighed at the confession, "Every day we wait is another day closer to whatever Keith's got planned, and it doesn't do us *or* Zane any good to wait."

They stared at her for a moment, startled by her revelation but nevertheless relieved to see her come to her senses.

"I just…" She shook her head and looked at Zoey with

pleading eyes. Zane had left her alone, and in his absence she was the one everyone looked to for guidance. She had unwillingly become their leader despite knowing nothing of ruling. "I can't do it alone."

Zoey gave her a nod, seeming to know exactly what was troubling her, and Serena wondered if she was reading her thoughts. "It's okay, Serena. I know this a lot to take on, but we're with you and able to help every step of the way."

Serena smiled and stood up, nodding, "Right. Then I guess we're doing this. No time like the present, right?"

"Damn straight!" Isaac smirked, slamming a fist into his palm, "I was getting a little stir-crazy in this hole!"

Zoey beamed at his excitement, obviously just as eager to be free of the lifeless, monochromatic abyss they'd condemned themselves to.

Serena smiled. Maybe she *could* do this. After all, she'd always refused to follow the orders of others, so why not be the one issuing the orders? She looked around, watching as everybody prepared; watching her clan prepare.

Her clan.

She smirked at the sound of it.

Though many had died and their headquarters had been destroyed, the Clan of Vail lived on and, despite Keith's plot to dismantle it and get its once proud followers executed in the process, she *would* lead them.

And she *would* win.

"Isaac! Round everyone up and make sure they understand the situation; anybody who wants out won't have the option later. Keith knows where we are and he'll think that gives him power! He's trying to motivate a response—something he can use as leverage with The Council to get things moving—and I'm sure he'll jump at the chance as soon as it presents itself. Everybody who chooses to fight with us should do what they need to prepare, I want to be ready to do this by tomorrow." She turned and faced Zoey, nodding to her friend as she fell into a comfortable place as their leader, "I need you to send him a message. If you project a psychic invitation to discuss the peaceful surrender of the clan then he'll be waiting like a kid at Christmas!"

"Surrender?" Isaac glared at her, "What are you saying?"

Serena smirked, "Not a gambler, are you?"

"A bluff?" Zoey frowned, "You're going to lie to get him out in the open?"

Isaac shook his head, "Isn't that a little underhanded? If he's looking to provide The Council with evidence that we've gone rogue won't that work to his advantage?"

"Short of killing him I don't think we can do much more to incriminate ourselves." Serena frowned, "He's made very sure to paint an ugly picture of us, and bitching and moaning won't make us look any prettier. He knows we've suffered a massive loss and he knows we're scared, and, in his mind, all we have left is a 'fight-or-flight' option; either we take him on and prove him right, or we give him what he wants and try to flee from a global force. He'll only come out from whatever rock he's hiding under if he thinks he stands to gain from it, and we're gonna use that for our advantage. I'm through playing fair, and tomorrow I'm showing Keith that he's not the only one that can fight dirty!"

The others nodded and smiled, obviously strengthened by her words and set about their tasks. Serena let out a heavy breath that she'd been holding during her entire speech and thanked Zane for giving her the strength to move forward with her life.

Retreating back to the room, she began raiding the dressers and closet—containing a mismatched assortment of clothes in random styles and sizes for whoever might have needed them—and snatched up a black, sleeveless top that barely fit around her chest and a pair of black leather pants that looked like something stolen from the set of a bad 80s movie. Deciding that it was the best she could hope for—and, in all fairness, she *could* make that shit work!—she set the outfit aside with her boots.

When there was nothing left to distract her from planning, she sighed and began to strategize. Keith had always been stronger than her. Even as kids she had never been able to match his speed or reflexes, and his auric control had always been spot-on where she had been forced to teach herself to direct her own aura through motions and lessons she'd learned from archery. And now...

She frowned and shook her head, not allowing herself to finish a thought that would only justify quitting.

Strength and speed weren't what would define this battle, anyway. Neither of them stood to gain anything in killing the other, outside of a warrant for their execution, and that shifted the nature of *how* they would fight.

The goal—for either side—was to incapacitate the other long enough for The Council to intervene.

And therein lay the second dilemma, *how* to get The Council's attention and lure them in to see Keith for who he really was.

She needed to play off her strengths; what she could do better than even Keith.

Then, as the solution dawned on her, she couldn't help but laugh.

With or without Zane, *this* was going to be epic.

Zane frowned as he continued through the mountainous terrain towards the caverns that the Taroe tribe that had cursed him once occupied, hoping that there might be some clue to his freedom in the remains. It had taken a lot of time and a lot of money to get him to that spot, and if he'd come all this way to find a dead end he didn't know what he'd do. He sighed, assuring himself that they'd be there as he continued pulling himself up the mountain; remembering the last time he'd been in this place.

Finally, he reached the hollowed-out entrance on the side of the slope and he groaned and heaved as the beast began to struggle. It didn't want to be there any more than he did. Being here was certain death for one, if not both, of them. The Taroe's magic surrounding the mountain sensed what was coming and made an effort to keep him out, and though it was a powerful spell and fighting it proved strenuous on his body, he was able to push through.

As he crossed the barrier's limit the spell released him and he fell forward as its grip on him vanished. Hitting the cave floor with a pained grunt, he started to pull himself up and found himself staring at a pair of ankles. Lifting his eyes towards the owner, he was both relieved and terrified to find a Taroe woman with long, red hair and bright green eyes that bore into him. Her tattoos—following the same tribal style of his own—were pale-white and contrasted against her dark skin.

"Looking for something, *Maledictus*?" she sneered.

"You?" he glared and shot to his feet, keeping his eyes on her, "Tell me there's a cure to these... these fucking things!" He gestured to his tattoos.

"A cure? For the tattoos; for the *curse*?" she scoffed. "Wouldn't be much of a curse if there were," she sneered, "And, like all tattoos, they're *permanent*!" She frowned as she watched him, her eyes almost searching him for something he couldn't name.

"Bullshit! Any other tattoos can be removed! Plenty have done it before! But *these*"—he slapped at the design on his arm and glared—"won't go away! I've been to *countless* places—traveled the fucking globe—to find somebody with a laser strong enough to burn your accursed ink from my skin, and *every* time I'd return home with them just as dark and crisp as the day you *fucks* put it in me!"

"Then why come to us now, *Maledictus*?"

Zane glared, "That's *not* my name!"

She chuckled, "That's funny, because it's written all over you!"

"That's not funny!" he snapped at her, taking another step.

"Then I am glad"—she sneered, not budging an inch—"that I was not *trying* to be!"

He growled and tried to step around her. If she wouldn't help him then he'd find the answers on his own. There had to be something that could undo his situation!

Anything!

She stepped to the side to block his efforts, "I've given you your answer, *Maledictus*! You earned those marks and the effects they have on you! You should feel honored!" She glared, "Nobody before you has *ever* worn the mark of *Maledictus*! You must be very proud of yourself! You've sealed your fate! Now leave!" She turned away from him.

"So why are you here? This tribe was destroyed years ago!" He narrowed his eyes and smirked, "I make a point of celebrating the anniversary of its destruction every year!"

"Perhaps I'm here to pay my condolences! You see, *Maledictus*, there *are* those who prefer to learn from the past and honor the lessons it offers us!" She sighed, "And what about you? Why come to a dead land looking for a cure you weren't even certain existed? Are you *really* so alone that you had nobody worth staying for?"

He clenched his teeth and looked away.

She nodded, smirking at him, "I see. You've come here not because you *are* alone, but because you are *not* alone! Can it be? Can *Maledictus*, a walking Apocalypse, *truly* change what it is simply because it *feels* for one of those suffering from its wrath?"

"It isn't like that!" He glared, "It's not *me* that's a threat to her!"

"Oh?" she raised an eyebrow, "And what makes her immune to the rage of *Maledictus*?"

He shook his head, "I… I don't know. She just is! It won't attack her! Hell, even its rage vanishes around her!"

Her eyes narrowed to slits, "You lie! *Maledictus* would never change its ways for anything or anyone!"

"Yea, I was pretty sure of that too, sweetheart!" Zane rolled his eyes, "I've been ready to wake up to find *everybody* dead—I've been *expecting* it!—so do you think that having my reality turned upside-down is a picnic for me?"

"Who are they? What are they to you?" she demanded, taking a step closer.

Zane stepped back, startled by her outburst, "I don't know!

Some chick! My old mentor's daughter!" He shook his head, "But even her old man couldn't sway the damn thing! There's no reason she should!"

"No..." She frowned, looking away, "*Maledictus* doesn't see a difference between friend or foe *or* their kin!"

"Then you see my problem, right? This broad's done the impossible! Tamed the savage dragon, soothed the raging beast! For fuck's sake, you said yourself that Melanoma—or whatever it is—doesn't *do* this sort of thing! So that means she's cracked the curse, right? Some sort of loophole in its design?"

"You're a fool!" She shook her head, "It doesn't work that way! The curse was created—*designed*—to make your life and the lives of those around you *miserable*! By sheer definition of the symbols you wear, none—no matter *who* they are or *what* they meant to you—should sway the—"

"Dammit, bitch! That's what I've been *saying*! Up until a few days ago she wasn't *anything* to me! I didn't know her. I didn't grow up with her. I haven't spent year-after-year pining and swooning and serenating this girl. *Nothing*!" Zane laughed as the tattoos started to tingle, "Oh, *that's* great! See what happened? You went and woke the baby!"

She rolled her eyes as her own tattoos began to glow and she focused on the searing red design visible on his arm, "*Superesse adhuc, Maledictus. Haec hora non indigetis videre ira tua.*"

Zane grimaced and shook as a tremor shook his body and then went still, his tattoos shifting back to normal. "What the..." He examined himself, "What the hell? In just a few days it's like everybody with a pair of tits can settle this thing down! What the fuck did you say?"

She exhaled slowly, letting her tattoos fade as well, "It's Latin. And I think I should come with you."

Zane stared at her in bewilderment, "Wh-what? What are you talking about? Why are you..." He shook his head, "Why should I take you *anywhere*?"

She stepped forward and, though she was noticeably smaller

than he was, seemed to overpower him with her stare alone, "Because if this girl *is* as special as you say—if she *does* have power over *Maledictus*—then you may already have your cure and you will need me to administer it."

Zane shook his head, "And why should I trust you? It was your people that did this to me in the first place! What happened to 'earning the marks' and all that shit?"

"Sometimes things change, Zane," she smirked, "And if both you *and Maledictus* can come to see the ugliness in yourselves and seek retribution for a noble cause, then perhaps the sentence can change as well."

Zane bit his lip and sighed, "If I find out you're fucking with me—"

"It is neither my nature nor my interest to deceive you!" She snapped, "So you can either accept my offer and bring me with you or you can carry on as you always have!"

Zane blushed at her fury, "Fair enough. So who are you, anyway?"

"My name's Nicc'oule, but the humans I trade with when I'm short on supplies call me Nikki."

He frowned, "You trade with humans? Do they know what you are?"

"They know that I am a woman," she responded, "and they know I am tattooed."

"Is that *all* they know?"

Nikki chuckled, "What more is there to know? I've had no reason to cast around them, so they have no reason to know I have magic, but just as you wear clothes to hide your nakedness, my decision to not reveal my magic does not mean that it is not there."

Zane narrowed his eyes, "Do they or do they *not* know *what* you are."

She scoffed and walked by him, "No, *Maledictus*. They do not."

Zane sighed and shook his head, turning to follow her, "Couldn't you have just *said* so? Was all that *really* necessary?"

"Nothing is necessary," she chuckled. "The decisions we make are motivated by circumstance and desire. We work so that we can afford to live. We bathe and make ourselves presentable so that we can attract a mate and start a family. And we act and behave as we do so that, when we die, we can be remembered."

Zane growled, "Okay... so what is the circumstances and desires behind all this cryptic bullshit?"

She laughed, "Because it is fun."

Zane stared after her, shaking his head. "Women..."

"This is taking too damn long," Zane grumbled, ignoring a brunette woman with a little kid standing in line ahead of them in the airport terminal. Lowering his voice he leaned towards Nikki, "Isn't there some—y'know?—*easier* way to get back?

Nikki frowned, "Easier than flying?"

"Yea..." He nodded towards her tattoos, "like teleporting or something like that."

"Teleporting?" she stared at him, "You want me to teleport us with my magic?"

Zane held his pointer finger to his lips and glared, "Yes, Miss Share-With-The-World! That's what I mean!"

"Like in the movies and on TV, right?"

"Uh... more or less, yea," Zane shrugged, "Is something wrong with that?"

Nikki rolled her eyes and turned to face him, "Okay, let me break down what you're asking me so that you can understand how stupid you sound. Now, you want *me*—somebody you've known only several hours and is more likely to *kill* you than offer kindness—to use *my* abilities to take *both* of us apart molecule-by-molecule. Then—now being *nothing* more than a microscopic jigsaw puzzle of myself—consciously direct *both* of us, in our molecular multitude, *hundreds* of miles away to a pinpoint location beyond sea, city, and forest that I've *never* been to and then, assuming that enough of me has survived this trip and is still actually all together and not spread out halfway across the planet, reassemble *both* of us into something *hopefully* resembling what we look like now. That about wrap up what you're asking of me?"

Zane shook his head at her, "Anybody ever tell you that you're a really abrasive fucking bitch sometimes?"

The brunette ahead of them whipped around and jabbed a sharp finger into Zane's face, "Excuse me!" She hissed at him, "There is a *child* here!"

Zane frowned and looked down at the little boy; shaggy brown hair, a hooded sweater that was several sizes too big for him, tiny jeans with the ghostly remnants of grass stains on the knees, and a pair of red Converse shoes that needed to be re-laced.

In a word: typical.

"Yes. Yes there *is* a child here! And I'm certain he'll even grow—as children have a way of doing, I've heard—into a young man, where he'll sprout some god-ugly acne and all sorts of body hair and start borrowing your fashion magazines for prolonged trips to the bathroom. Then, when he's done pumping protein into *every* piece of fabric in your home, maybe he'll march off to college and, if he's miraculously avoided knocking up some future pole-dancer, maybe even get a job that *won't* leave him selling drugs to make rent on a crappy studio apartment. Shit, lady, he may even grow up to be *president* some day! So bravo, toots, you've reproduced. Now, while I thank you for showing me that there is, indeed, a child present, I'm going to return to the conversation I *was* having and *you're* going to turn around and shut your fucking mouth!"

The woman's eyes grew wider and wider with every sentence as her jaw dropped lower and lower. By the time Zane had finished he wasn't sure if she was going to attack him, or if her head would just pop off her shoulders from sheer rage. Fortunately for both of them, her son, having overheard the rant but not understanding most of it, provided a distraction:

"Wow, Mommy! Can I *really* be president some day?"

The woman, still shaking with rage and barely registering her son's words, shook her head. "No, Eric! Don't listen to a word he says! He's a crazy ma—" then, suddenly realizing what she was saying, turned to the boy as the first wave of tears cascaded down his cheeks and he ran away from her with a shriek.

Firing Zane one final death glare, the woman sacrificed her spot in line and began running after her traumatized son.

Zane smirked and stepped forward to the now-open spot.

Nikki, frowning at him, shook her head as she stepped up beside him. "That was *horrible!*"

"I agree," Zane nodded, "No parent should discourage their kid like that."

"You know what I mean!" She looked past him towards where they had run off to, "I just don't see how you find that funny."

Zane shrugged, "Serena would've thought it was a riot."

Nikki frowned and stared at him, "Is that the one you were talking about? The one that calms *Maledictus?*"

Zane nodded.

"So what do you know about her?" Nikki asked.

Zane sighed, "I know that she's stubborn and arrogant and obnoxious and an overall pain in the ass!"

Nikki raised an eyebrow, "And *this* is the woman that soothes—"

"In my defense, I *did* already point out that it makes *no* goddam sense!"

"But..." She shook her head, "But there must be *something* about her! Some goodness or sincerity or affection or magic!"

Zane shook his head, "Only magic with that woman is how she can bust my balls over and over again and *still* irritate the shit out of me every time she opens her mouth."

Nikki laughed and smiled, "I like her already!"

"Yea," he groaned, pinching the bridge of his nose and advancing as the line moved ahead, "I'm sure you two will hit it off just great! She's already turned one of my clan mates to the dark side, too!"

"Well at least she's making friends, right?" Nikki smiled, "So what's your clan mate like? Are they romantic with one another?"

Zane laughed, "I severely doubt it! Though I wouldn't mind seeing *that!*"

Nikki frowned in confusion.

"My clan mate's a *girl*, Nikki. Her name's Zoey, and I don't think she *or* Serena swing that way."

"So you *are* in love with her!" Nikki chided.

"I'm not..." He sighed, "It's not as simple as that! Sure, there's something there, but there's a big fucking mess in the middle of it all."

"A mess?" Nikki frowned, "What sort of mess?"

"Like the ex-boyfriend-slash-fiancé sort of mess!" Zane sneered.

"Oh. Is he trying to get her back?"

Zane shook his head, "Not anymore. Your precious curse saw to that."

Nikki looked around to make sure nobody was listening before responding: "She's still interested in you after you *killed* her previous lover?"

Zane growled and shook his head, "No, dammit! It's not... he was *already* dead!"

Nikki stared at him, "But you just said—"

"I know what I said, okay! I even know how it sounds! But ever since I found her and her phantom baggage it's become normal, everyday bullshit! Just one more way for her to drive me up the fucking wall!"

"A 'phantom'? You mean her lover? He was a *ghost?* Then how did you"—she looked around again and lowered her voice—"how could you kill him if he was already dead?"

Zane narrowed his eyes at her, "Did I stutter, Nikki? I. Don't. Know! He was trying to possess me so he could have my body to be with her again. Halfway through the process our angry friend came in and ripped his aura to pieces."

Nikki studied him, "You can do that?"

"Apparently," Zane glared, "I wasn't exactly asking for a

physics lesson while I did it! One moment his aura was there—working *very* hard to steal my body—and the next he wasn't."

"Then the *Maledictus* reacted to protect your body from being taken?"

"I guess so," Zane frowned, "But I'm not about to *thank* it if that's what you're saying."

"No, I wasn't going to say that," Nikki said, turning her head to watch a plane taking off through the window.

Zane looked over, "Then what *were* you going to say?"

Nikki was silent as she watched the plane lift off the ground before turning away and looking back at Zane, "I was going to ask if that had ever happened before?"

"What do you mean?"

Nikki sighed, "You said that Serena's dead lover—as an aura—tried to take control of your body; to *possess* you so that he and Serena could be together again."

Zane nodded, "Yes. That *is* what I just said. What's your point?"

"My point," Nikki said, narrowing her eyes at him, "is to find out if he'd ever done something like that before!"

CHAPTER THIRTEEN
BOILING OVER

THE 24-HOUR WINDOW THAT SERENA had given the others to make their decisions was nearly up, and while she was confident in her strategy and hopeful of the overall plan, her nerves had kept her from getting too much rest. Despite what was coming, she was surprised to find the majority of her fragmented sleep interrupted and haunted by thoughts and chaotic dreams of Zane. At times she'd feel as though he was beside her—his tattooed skin only inches from her body—and she found herself waking up to try to move closer to him only to be reminded that she was alone. Scenarios played out within her, refusing to let her mind slip into unconsciousness for hours at a time, and entire conversations—supportive and loving as well as scornful and enraged—were scripted from start to finish. In every case that she imagined, no matter how they entered into the conversation, it ended in the same way. This thought, again and again, was carried with her into what sleep she was offered, and her dreams became an erotic flurry that enacted what she had, in her waking moments, led up to. Then, drenched from both sweat and arousal, she'd awaken, certain that Zane was lying beside her.

And the cycle would begin once again.

Finally, fed up with being teased by her own subconscious, she decided to punish her own depraved mind by refusing to let it titillate her any longer with broken promises of sleep. Instead, in an effort to focus her mind, she followed the route Zoey had shown her earlier to the munitions room and began to explore the collection of high-powered weapons. Though most of them were far more complex and a great deal larger than anything she'd ever handled, she still found herself feeling more and more comfortable with the idea of strolling onto the battlefield with one of the impressive guns slung over her shoulder. As the range of firearms increased in size the deeper she explored the room, she became evermore enticed by them; the fantasy of toting a shiny automatic weapon that was longer than she was tall and sporting a belt of ammunition that stretched for nine yards.

She smirked at the idea of unloading *that* into the wide-eyed Keith's chest.

The whole nine yards!

She laughed to herself as she ran her palm over the cool metal surface, reminding herself once again that killing was not an option, and moved on to the next violent fantasy.

Despite all the ogling and fantasizing, Serena found that she'd only been able to kill forty minutes in her excursion. Carrying a few of the more modest and "less lethal"—as she'd been able to convince herself—guns from the room in a duffle bag, she started back for her room to think of her *next* mundane distraction.

And then she saw her!

The length of the tunnel Serena was walking through centered her on the end as she looked around the main corridor; clearly lost. Though she was still a ways away, Serena could see that the strange woman—with skin like milk chocolate and bright red hair—was *not* one of Vail's warriors *or* a part of Isaac's pack!

And that narrowed her list of potential comrades to only one other that knew their location...

Keith!

As the intruder continued to peer down the numerous passageways, still oblivious that she had been spotted, Serena set down the duffle bag and reached in for the first available gun.

Suddenly "less lethal" was no longer a concern.

She wanted something—anything!—that was a part of Keith and his bullshit *dead*!

Pulling out the first gun her hand touched, she frowned at the strange design. All her life it had been the simple, small things; two parts that mattered: trigger and barrel. One you pulled, the other killed what it was aimed at. Simple! What she held now was at least two-times longer and far heavier than anything her father had shown her before she'd left the clan.

Suddenly she wished she'd paid more attention to what he'd been saying instead of waiting for archery practice.

The handle and trigger she recognized; simple and where it belonged. Good!

The barrel, though a lot more intimidating than what she had seen before, still faced forward when the handle and trigger were held as she'd been shown; the length made aiming a little more complicated, but still familiar. Excellent!

Then there was all this shit in between the two; shit that looked important: complicated, foreign, confusing.

"Fuck," she grumbled, trying to decipher the gun's components by glaring at it. Suddenly she remembered what she'd been doing and looked up towards the corridor again.

The stranger was gone!

Serena frowned, "Double-fuck!"

Clutching the gun, she shot down the hall and into the corridor and spotted the intruder as she peered down one of the other tunnels. As she glared, Serena felt her fangs extend and she began to shiver with the anticipation of the impending fight. Suddenly, as though hearing her excitement, the woman turned and looked at her, smirking as she spotted her.

"Ah! You must be Serena!" She turned and started towards her.

Serena's eyes widened at the advance and she whipped the gun forward and held it how she assumed she was supposed to, hoping to catch the intruder off guard long enough to plan an attack that relied less on the mechanics of a military weapon.

The woman's green eyes went wide and her hands went up as she took a step back, "Whoa! Okay! Bad start! I'm—"

Serena hissed, "I know who sent you!"

"Who sent me?" she frowned and shook her head, "Look, you're confused. I'm sorry if I startled you, but Zane was—"

"Zane?" Serena's eyes widened. This woman—this *bitch*—knew Zane? How? If Keith was sending his subordinates to them then he must have captured Zane! She snarled and threw down the gun and charged the woman, "Where is he, you bitch?"

"No! Wai—"

Serena slammed into her, knocking them both to the ground as she reached out with her aura and pinned her down, holding her fists up and baring her fangs, "Tell me where he is or I swear I'll fucking—"

"Didn't I tell you she was a charmer, Nikki?" Zane's voice echoed down the passage as he descended the ladder. "I swear, Serena! *This* is why we can't have guests over! 'Hi, nice to meet you! How was your day? Let me take your coat. Hope you don't mind if I eat your face'" he shook his head and chuckled.

Serena's eyes widened as her aura deflated and withdrew into her still chest as she struggled to remember how to breathe. "Z-Zane? You... you're here. You came back!"

Zane nodded, "Well yea! What? A guy can't go on a calm relaxing stroll without panicking the little lady?"

Serena glared, "You were gone for *four* fucking days!"

"Yea..." Zane rubbed the back of his neck, "Sometimes calm and relaxing strolls are more like trips to other continents and dangerous hikes up unexplored, mountainous terrain. To-may-to, to-mah-to, right?"

"You ass-hat!" Serena threw herself off the still-shocked woman and drove her knee into Zane's stomach and brought an elbow into his solar plexus, "You *left* us here with *no* idea of *where* you were or *when* you're dumb ass was planning to come back! I thought you were *dead*, you inconsiderate fuck!"

Zane heaved and keeled over as he dropped to his knees, "N-nice... to see... you too!"

Serena glared down at him, "You're lucky my ass doesn't know how to work that piece-of-shit gun or I'd shoot you in the dick!"

"Glad to see..." He groaned and curled tighter into the fetal position and began to cough, "... I'm one of the fortunate ones."

The woman that Zane had called Nikki stood and frowned, looking down at Zane as he writhed about in pain.

"Incredible! The magic isn't even awakening!"

Serena looked over, still breathing heavily from the rush of adrenaline, "What are you talking about?"

Nikki knelt down and pointed at Zane's tattoos, "See? They're still black! Not even a spark! After something like that the *Maledictus* would have taken over—*should* have taken over—but there's nothing!"

Serena sneered, "What's this about Megatron taking over?"

Though he was still groaning in pain, Zane started laughing only to cringe and clutch his stomach tighter, "Oh! Damn!"

Nikki blushed, standing up, "The *Maledictus*; the curse! The beast that he turns into!"

"That thing has a name?" Serena frowned.

Nikki shrugged, "More-or-less." She shook her head, "No matter what you call it, it *should* be on a rampage after the beating you just gave him." Staring at Zane's tattoos a moment longer she chuckled, "I wouldn't have believed it in a *million* years! You really do calm it!"

Serena shook her head and shot another glare at Zane, "Doesn't have a thing to do with 'calm'! Damn thing *knows* better than to show itself right now or I'd hand it its own ass, too!"

It took nearly an hour for Zane to coax Serena's voice to a normal volume and pitch, but in that time he wasn't able to keep her from hurting him any further beyond the occasional slap when she was forced to pause long enough to draw a breath.

"Look," Zane sighed when the rage in Serena's eyes dimmed and turned to sadness, "I'm sorry that I made you worry. After I left, I realized that what we needed—what I *wanted*—was to be able to live *without* worrying about that goddam monster fucking up everything anytime I got upset. I've tried so many times to have the tattoos removed or the curse lifted; been to doctors, cosmetic surgeons, fortune-tellers, mediums, and enough aurics to repopulate those we lost the other day! But nothing works! The tattoos won't come off and the magic in them has fused to my cells! I'm not even sure *dying* will work at this point or if I'd just be handing control over to it for good."

"Why? Why does it matter who or what you are? You've known for so long that they couldn't remove the tattoos!" Serena frowned, slumping down on the bed beside him, "I understand that it's important to you to *not* to be a monster for my sake or the sake of Zoey and the others! But did you ever stop and think that disappearing like that might hurt us *more*? I mean, maybe I *like* you the way you are! Did you ever think of that? Maybe you aren't as bad as you or everybody else or even the *curse* says you are! Have you ever *once* looked in the mirror and *realized* that, behind all the fireworks and special effects, these are *still* just tattoos? And, let's be honest for a moment, it's not like they're hard on the eyes;

pretty far from it, actually!"

Zane gave her a look, "You can't be serious!"

Serena smirked, "What? You don't believe me?" She shook her head and stuck her tongue out, "Girls *love* sexy men with ink!"

Zane raised an eyebrow, "So you're calling me 'sexy'?"

Serena smacked him again, "Don't be a prepubescent bitch-boy, Zane! We're not in middle school and you're not asking me to some spring formal!"

"Yea," Zane frowned, rubbing his shoulder, "I'll try to remember that. And I guess I see your point—about the tattoos and all, at least—but it just… well, it *sucks*! I'm not gonna sugarcoat it; it hurts so fucking bad, and I don't know how much more fucking stress my body can handle before…" He sighed and hung his head, "I don't like not knowing how much longer I've got."

"Yea, because I wake up every morning knowing *exactly* how long I've got before I go tits-up!"

Zane frowned, "'tits-up'?"

"Grow up, dick! You *know* what I mean! The point is that *nobody* knows when they'll die! Some are given days and march on for years, and others who are seen as the fittest and finest end up choking on a damn Tic-Tac!" She shook her head at him, "You think everybody with some condition that *might* end their lives use it as an excuse *not* to live?"

Zane bit his lip and looked down, "I guess. It's just scary to think that I might lose myself to that thing."

Serena smiled and set her hand on his knee, "I won't let it take you over. We'll work together and you'll get better. Even if you can't cure it, you can learn to control it more."

Considering this for a moment, Zane shifted his eyes to her hand on his leg—feeling the warmth and comfort from her palm starting to send ripples through his body—and realized it was the first time that a woman had touched him out of genuine affection and not just because he'd paid them or because they were afraid of him.

And he didn't want it to stop there.

Not now.

"Serena…" He looked up at her, studying her and trying to see if her expression might answer the burning question. Even then, seeing her stare back at him without fear or repulsion, he couldn't be certain. It had just been too damn long!

"It's alright, Zane," Serena assured him, her ruby lips curling up in an irresistible grin, "I'll *never* be done getting under your skin."

Zane felt his body go hot, and, though he felt a well of terror initially, he realized that, for the first time in a long time, it had nothing to do with the curse. "I want…" he scowled at the way it sounded and shook his head, "No! I *need* to touch you."

Her smile didn't waver or shift as her eyes shifted to his mouth and she moistened her lips, "then what's stopping you?"

And suddenly his fear was gone.

God damn if she didn't do it again!

Smirking at the bizarre power she had over him, he pushed her to her back with one arm while using the other to pull her face to his, finally getting a chance to taste and feel her. That contact, like the first drop of blood on a parched tongue, sparked a raw need that transcended any previous desires.

Suddenly *any* distance between them—any part of her that wasn't held against him—was an even greater curse than any of the tattoos had ever been or could hope to be!

Suddenly the deaths of many and the destruction of all were distant concerns when compared to the collapse of the current moment.

Suddenly he understood.

Struggling to pull his lips from hers, he looked into her face, seeing her for everything she was and would be from that moment on.

"What?" she smiled and started to move her face towards his again.

"You…" he blushed as she paused to hear what he had to say, "you loved me."

She smirked, "Dummy. I still do!"

He shook his head, "no. Before—back in the forest that night—you *showed* me love; showed *him* love."

She blinked and leaned back, "what do you mean?"

He smiled, "that first night... I couldn't remember what had happened; how we ended up waking up together like that."

Serena blushed at the mention of that night and she began to stammer, "I... I'm sorry. Devon and I nee—"

Zane's smile widened and he squeezed her hand, "No, I know, now! I *understand*, Serena! Devon possessed me—took control of my body so you two could have a physical moment—and, in doing so, you showed me—my body and the curse *tied* to my body— something that I've *never* had; something that the curse was never 'programmed' to understand!"

Serena stared at him, blushing and smiling, "Then you..."

He nodded, "I *remember* that night! Remember *letting* Devon in; letting him control us... because of how you looked at us. The curse was made to destroy and cause suffering! It was never supposed to *get* far enough with another to have what you gave us that night!" He beamed, "You—your *love*—*is* the reason you can control it! You are a *cure* to the rage!"

She blushed, arching an eyebrow, "Oh? And what does that mean for us now? With me being a cure, and all?"

He stared at her a moment longer and smiled, letting his hand trace over her cheek, "It means that, right now, I'm taking my first dose of a lifetime remedy!" His hand found her shoulder and pulled her into him once again as he slammed his lips to hers and taking in all of her essence with a greater understanding of what it meant.

Moaning, Serena lifted her chin more to match his efforts and deepened the kiss. Neither of them were used to giving in; had never backed down in a challenge, and it showed then and there. For every ounce of pressure one put in, the other matched and surpassed. Their combined efforts—a violent eruption of passion and desire and need—had them clawing each other's clothes from their bodies in a mad-dash effort to rid themselves of *anything* that could come between them.

As the last burden of fabric was cast away they began to worship every inch of the other's skin; nipping at necks and kissing along the length of exposed shoulders and down further to flesh that, despite the rising heat, had become tight and puckered. Their senses were overwhelmed by the sound of their racing hearts and the torrents of blood coursing through veins and further fueling their mutual need.

Serena groaned as his mouth paid homage to her heaving chest and she moved her hand along his side until she had his length throbbing in the palm of her hand. The sexual energies increased as their contact grew. Zane gasped at the contact, his warm breath rushing over the lingering moisture his kisses had left on her chest and causing her to shiver and writhe beneath him.

Not ready to give him his victory, she met his passion with her own; pumping her hand along her prize and biting her lip as she watched his face shift into a mask of ecstasy; the first bead of moisture surfacing against her palm and trailing back down its length.

Refusing to succumb entirely to her skills, he countered her touch with his own; letting the fingertips of his right hand trace down her stomach and into her depths. Heat and moisture enveloped his advances and he felt his breath catch in his chest as he watched Serena's face wash over with pleasure as she leaned her head back in a silent moan and exposed her throat in its entirety to him. And, though he ached to taste more of her—to take more of her into him—he was more driven, at that moment, to fill her with himself instead.

No longer able to keep score over whose passion had tipped the scale, they offered one another a silent draw as their mouths found one another again and they became one.

CHAPTER FOURTEEN
ANTICIPATION

NIKKI SIGHED AS SHE WATCHED the group finalize their plan against the Keith-vampire that had seemed to make quite an impression on *all* of them.

Though she and the rest of her tribe had never had much direct business with The Council, she understood that there had long-since been a shaky truce between them and all Taroe, who—because of their practices and knowledge—posed a potential threat to the Mythos community's secrecy, which, from what Nikki had gathered, was a key motivator to most of the laws they worked so hard to uphold. In this regard, however, she was in understanding, since her people had always thrived *because* of the fact that they hid their activities from the humans. While there was nothing inherently inhuman about her or any other Taroe—who, though she hated to admit it, were *still* just humans with an advanced understanding of magic—their paranormal activities were enough to draw the attention of the supernatural creatures who valued secrecy and ambiguity as much as they did. Still, while The Council's affairs had never *directly* impacted her, she was very aware of the power they wielded and what that power meant for every living being on the planet; human or Mythos.

A power, it turned out, that Keith was using for selfish and vengeful purposes. And while she hardly considered herself an expert in the subject, it was worked into the minds of every Taroe youth that entered into adulthood with the tattooing rites that power of *any* kind should never be wielded in such ways.

It was why the *Maledictus* curse had never been used before— or after—Zane had brought it down on himself.

An act, ironically enough, that brought The Council down on their tribe.

Just like the elders had warned; power wielded against somebody in anger will only bring anger back upon them.

And though she was supportive of their goals, she could not will herself to be interested in the tedious planning process they were applying to it. As the group's incessant banter cycled back and began again she tried to hold back a yawn.

And failed.

"Is something boring to you?" Serena asked, lifting her eyes to her.

Nikki frowned as the attention of the room turned to her, "I just feel like you're thinking about this *way* too much."

Serena frowned, "You're saying we *shouldn't* plan our approach?"

"I'm not saying *not* to plan," she offered, "So much as I'm saying you might not want to make your plans so rigid. You can plan for *years* on how to react to an attack from the front, but if, when the day comes to fight, you're attacked from the *side*, then you wasted all that time and focus on something that didn't allow for any adaptation. Furthermore, if you're dealing with a *perfect* vampire—who can use his aura to *read* your thoughts *and* attack with the speed and strength of a sang—then would it *really* be in all of your best interests to walk in with everyone *thinking* the same thing?"

A collective frown washed over the room as everyone realized that what she said was right. Though she had successfully shifted the judgment on her, she nevertheless resisted the urge to jump onto the table to do a victory dance, knowing that it would only serve to reverse what she'd just achieved.

"So, what would you suggest then, Nikki?" Zane glared, stepping behind Serena and setting his hand on her shoulder.

Nikki frowned and felt her chest tighten as the tension rose, but forced herself to shrug it off, "Well, I haven't known any of you for very long, but I see no reason why you shouldn't be able to handle yourselves using your natural abilities. It looks like you all understand the situation and how you want things to turn out, so why shouldn't you all be able to do what's come natural for so long?" She smirked, "Besides, it's not like he or his followers can plan any more than you can, since both of you"—she nodded towards Serena and Zoey—"can 'see' their thoughts just as easily. Plus, and I hate to be the one to say this, but you *do* have your ace-in-the-hole."

Zane frowned at her, "And what would that be?"

Nikki bit her lip as she watched him brace himself for what he knew was coming and she sighed, "You, Zane. If it gets too bad out there, *Maledictus* will do what it's made to do."

A deep, rumbling growl started in Zane's chest and started up his throat. Just before his lips had a chance to part to let it out, Serena's hand raised and came to rest on his sternum, stifling his growing rage and muting the encroaching snarl in the process. Startled, he looked at her, uncertainty warping his enraged features.

Serena smiled warmly at him and nodded, "They're *just* tattoos,

Zane. Don't let *them* wear *you*."

Zane bit his lip, "But we can't just—"

Serena increased the pressure on his chest, "We will do whatever works for us." She looked at Nikki and smiled, "I remember, when we were still young, playing in these woods with Keith. One of my favorite things to do was play a game called 'stronghold'. Keith *hated* the game not only because he could never win, but because it was also the *only* thing I beat him in *every* time." She leaned forward and nodded at Nikki, "Now, the rules of 'stronghold' were simple: we each built a small structure—our personal strongholds—with materials we found around the woods. We would pick different spots to build on to try and vary the outcome, but it never worked for Keith. You see, once we were finished building our strongholds, Keith got to send an auric blast at both of them. Just one blast against both structures—the *same* force against both of them—and the winner was whoever's stronghold was the *least* destroyed.

"What you just said about not relying on a single, reinforced plan reminds me a lot of why I always beat Keith. Even as a kid Keith was all about strength and rigidity—I swear he was *born* with a stick up his ass!—but I knew that when his aura hit our strongholds, that if anything was too stiff, it would drag everything else with it. He could *never* figure out why his strongholds—which were built from the thicker, harder branches and always bound tighter and tighter and built taller and taller with each new game— toppled every time and mine—built with thinner and more flexible branches that I wove loosely in a pyramid shape—hardly shifted under the force of his aura." She laughed, "He actually started throwing harder and harder blasts, and while he *did* start causing some damage to my stronghold, his would be *demolished!*"

Zane looked over at her, "Serena?"

She beamed brighter and nodded, "I like you, Nikki! You're not afraid to call an entire room on their bullshit *and* prove them wrong in doing so. And, though he hates it, Zane's situation *can* help us in a pinch. No matter how hard my asshole of a brother and his followers hit us, if we can hit him just as hard and be more flexible while doing it, then none of them will be left standing. My father once told me that what separates a *good* leader from a *great* leader lies between knowing you're good enough and admitting when others are better."

Zane and the rest of the room stared at her in shock.

Nikki blushed, "What are you saying?"

Serena smiled and nodded, "I'm saying that when we step out there to do what we need to do, I want you to lead us. I'm saying that I want you to be our general!"

"Ah! It feels so good to have a place to work out again!" Nikki mused to herself as she stepped into the training room where a few of the therions of Isaac's pack were weight-training. As she started to get settled in, however, their activities fizzled until they just stood and watched her begin to stretch with a little too much interest. Smiling at the attention, she turned to them and winked, "Sorry, boys. I'm still getting over my *last* therion lover."

They groaned and scowled as they moved on to other activities and Nikki smirked before she channeled her energies around her and began to throw her empowered punches and kicks into a reinforced punching bag.

"That thing is going to get *demolished* by the time you're done!" The therion named Isaac mused as he paused from his sparring with the vampire named Zoey long enough to watch her assault on the sandbag. Nikki had noticed the two had been really close since she had gotten there.

She shrugged and drove her fist into it once more, "Better it than me, right?" She grinned.

Turning back to the sandbag, she narrowed her eyes at it, imagining Zane's face for a moment before driving her fists into the center of the bag repeatedly.

"Nikki, we need your help with the plans," Zane called out as he stepped into the room.

"What plans? I thought we'd decided *against* too much planning!" She shook her head and sighed, sending another powerful punch into the center of the training bag.

"Please refrain from destroying our equipment. It's not made for your type of magic," Zane sighed.

She smirked, noticing that a few of the supporting rails above her had begun to warp, "Didn't know I was *that* strong! You should probably invest in stronger equipment." She rolled her eyes and turned to Zane. She could certainly see the appeal that the Serena girl saw in him, he wasn't a *total* loss in the looks department; though it didn't change the fact that he was a grade-A asshole. Still, she *could* get used to the face and body.

Besides, it wasn't him she liked.

"So what do you need?" she asked.

"It's this whole Keith mess," he answered flatly.

As if it was ever that simple, she sighed. "Oh? You sound like you have something in mind."

"Not particularly, but if you're going to be leading us then I'd like to know what *you* had in mind."

Nikki smiled and looked at the punching bag and shrugged, "Well, one of the benefits of being what I am is knowing that very few understand what they're dealing with. A human would think I was a monster and a Mythos would think I was nothing more than a human," she smirked over at him knowingly, "So, at any point in a battle, I'm either against somebody who's either *already* afraid of me, or underestimating me."

Zane frowned, "Is there a point to this? I'd like to get back to Serena soon."

"Oh I won't be long," Nikki chuckled, throwing a gentle punch into the sandbag, "Anyway, what I've come to learn from this is that—afraid or unafraid—it's never hard to get the enemy to get sloppy. Either their nerves get to them and you get them desperate *not* to die"—she drove several more punches into the sandbag—"*or* they shift their focus because they're certain they've already won." Zane frowned as she continued to throw her magic-laced punches and began to mix some kicks into her approach and the sandbag continued to shift and pitch under the impacts, "Either way, when the opposition gets sloppy, their hold on the situation gets weaker and weaker until…" She drove her fist into the sandbag, letting it swing out before driving her leg into the side and tearing it from the ceiling and sending it crashing to the floor and spilling sand all over the gymnasium.

Zane sighed, staring at the mess and looking up at her, "You know you're paying for that, right?"

Nikki smirked, "I'll make you a deal, *Maledictus*; if I succeed in leading you and the others in tomorrow's battle then consider me settled up. Otherwise, I'll pay *ten* times the damages!"

"If you fail," Zane frowned, "we'll be *dead*."

Nikki smirked and patted his shoulder, "Like I said; consider me settled up."

Zane sighed as he stepped through the door to his and Serena's room, grumbling as he locked up.

Serena smirked and looked up at him from the bed, her purple eyes meeting his mismatched bright gaze, "That didn't take you long."

"She broke a sandbag and told me to bill her…"

Serena giggled, "Well, at least she's taking responsibility, right?"

Zane sighed and shook his head, "Yea… *if* we die!"

Serena cackled.

"Yea, it's hilarious," Zane sighed, "You and her are clearly *made* for each other!"

"Well, as true as that might be," she smirked, "she's missing a few things that I'm looking for in a lover."

"Oh?" His eyes sparked and he studied her shape under the sheets with refreshed interest.

Serena smirked, seeing him stare and she shifted to give him a better view of her, "Oh my, Zane. Are you ready for *another* go, again?"

"What? Is five times too many?" Zane gave a phony pout as he walked towards the bed.

Serena smiled and started to peel her shirt off, "Don't worry, baby. I'll tell you when you've had enough."

"And if you can't stop me after that?" He smirked and leaned closer, kissing her neck causing her to gasp.

"Mmm! I don't know. I don't think I could say 'no' even if I wanted to," she confessed, smirking.

He smirked and continued to kiss lower, "Then I guess I have nothing to worry about."

"You know me," she groaned as his lips traced her naval, "I... I aim to please."

Zane grinned and reached down, "Oh? You too? Then maybe you can tell me how my aim is." She moaned loudly as he found his mark and bit her lip, "Oh! Looks like I'm still an expert marksman," he smirked.

Tired of the games, Serena pulled him down and wrapped herself around him.

CHAPTER FIFTEEN
A GAME OF "STRONGHOLD"

THE FOREST WAS COLD AND QUIET in the throes of dusk, even more so than usual. With a low-hanging cloud of mist turning the landscape into a haunted haze, Zane and Serena and the rest of their small, lackluster army of surviving Vail warriors marched together in the clearing.

There was no question if Keith and his group were there—of that they were all certain—but the atmosphere and his auric shields made knowing his exact location and intentions impossible.

Serena frowned as she felt the first wave of doubt rift through their ranks and she looked over at Zane. "Do you think this will work, Zane?"

Zane nodded, his familiar warrior swagger throwing extra power behind each step he took, "No worries, babe! We got this one in the bag!" He sighed and looked forward. "It's like Nikki said; we're covered for the worst," he lingered on that thought a moment before he looked back and smirked at her, "Besides, you *do* have your one, *unmistakable* talent."

Serena smirked, remembering her discussion earlier with Zane pertaining to the skill that had rapidly made her an iconic force— one that trumped Keith, Zane, Devon, and *any* other who dared to try their luck with her—and made her nothing short of *legendary* in her applications...

Her uncanny ability to piss *anybody* off!

She laughed again and flipped her hair proudly as Zane reminded her of just how skilled she had become at getting under the skin of anybody in her path, and while she thought—hell, she goddam *knew*!—that Zane hadn't simply agreed to this revelation for her sake, she hoped that the "gift" wouldn't fail her when it counted for something more than a petty argument.

"Damn-straight, it's gonna work!" Nikki grinned as her tattoos began to shimmer with the promise of battle as she peered through the rows of trees and pulled out two Sais, rolling the forked swords in each palm to check their balance one last time.

At an unspoken cue, the group stopped their advance in the center of the clearing and prepared themselves for what was next. Isaac and the rest of the therions had already transformed and, as they saw the vampires give the signal and prepare their weapons, their bestial forms shifted into view from the trees and surrounding landscape and they moved forward to join them.

"Well well well, Serena! *This* is quite an unconventional way to begin a *negotiation*, wouldn't you say?" Keith snickered as he stepped out of the fog ahead of them, arms held out and palms empty as he stepped confidently towards them, "Guns? Swords? *Therions?*" He shook his head and clucked his tongue, "If I was a less-trusting type I might be worried that I'd been tricked; maybe even go so far as to claim that I'd been deceived! This, however, would be *beyond* foolish and you—my dear, sweet, naïve bitch-of-a-sister—are certainly nobody's fool."

Zane bared his fangs and hissed angrily, "Watch your mouth, you bastard, or you can *watch* me rip it from you!"

"Oh my!" Keith held a hand to his chest in mock-horror, "Such brash words and barbaric threats! Perhaps I *should* reconsider my stance on how to deal with our father's treachery and the blind support of the morons he kept company with!" He took another step forward and smirked at Zane, arching an eyebrow, "How well *did* you know him, Zane? What *was* it that Gregori told you that you're so quick to accept at face value?" he snorted and shook his head. "Now, *I'm* willing to wager it's something to the tune of: 'Keith is mad with power' and 'he's deceiving The Council' and whatnot, am I right?" He smirked at Serena, "Do *you* think that they're stupid, Serena? Would you say—here and now and with all of these witnesses to hear it—that *The* Mythos Council are *imbeciles?*"

Serena glared, "You know I wouldn't!"

"Oh ho? You would be *right* about that, too! Because they *aren't* idiots!" He laughed and turned his back on them, his voice echoing around them as he continued to rant like a lawyer on his closing statement, "So, now that we're in agreement as to the credibility of my employers, is it fair to assume that *I* am the monster that you so obviously appear to be convinced I am? Or, and bear with me here, does it seem more likely that, upon my *leaving* our father's clan— upon seeing his corrupt and foolish use of The Council's support—that he would *lie* to his mindless drones to maintain their trust?" he paused and glanced over his shoulder at Zane. "So, my bestial bastard half-brother, just *how* well did you *know* my and Serena's father?"

Zane's eyes had narrowed into angry slits as his jaw shifted and clenched, his tattoos beginning to glow. Seeing this, Nikki's tattoos flared as she began to chant under her breath and Serena watched as wisps of her pale aura began to work their soothing magic on him.

Frowning, Serena looked back at Keith and shook her head, "You always did love to talk." She sneered, "But do you expect *me*—one who grew up beside you and knew him better than *anybody* else here could hope to!—to abandon what I *know* just because you can weave a fancy sentence and"—she glared and threw her aura out in a pulsing wave throughout the clearing and shattering his auric shields and, with them, his psychic influences on their group—"*fuck* with peoples' minds?" She glared at him as the group began to realize their minds had been tampered with, "Now, Keith—my ass-kissing, limp-dick, parasitic *worm* and shitty excuse for a brother—if you'll be so kind as to *repeat* your speech *without* your eel-like aura slithering through my friends' minds?"

Keith hissed at her, "Bitch!"

Serena smirked, "I've been called *far* worse by *far* better, shit-stain!"

"How *dare*—" Keith stopped himself and breathed in, steadying his thrashing aura and calming himself before offering a solemn nod. "It can't be said that I didn't try with you, Serena." He glared at her, "As much as I'm sure you'll tell them otherwise when you're suffering The Council's wrath! I come here *alone* to peacefully negotia—"

"Oh, eat shit and rot, you lying cock-stain! I *know* you brought others!" Serena glared, stepping forward and swiftly drawing back and firing an auric bow in a fluid motion that caught Keith off guard. As the bright purple tendril cut through the clearing and slammed into Keith's leg, knocking him to one knee, the blinding fog broke and revealed the waiting army that Keith had brought. She smirked, keeping her auric grip on her brother's leg, "And now everyone else does, too." She shook her head at him, "Are there any more lies you want to try to feed us before I wipe the woods with you?"

"Oh no, sis," Keith laughed and wrapped a pair of red auric "arms" around Serena's hold on him and easily crushed it, "I think it's safe to assume that everything worth saying has been said!" ·

Serena cried out as the energy backlash hit and she fell to the ground.

Zane's eyes flashed and he snarled and shot at Keith, his aura beginning to shift from blue-to-red. Seeing his advance, Keith's aura surrendered its hold on Serena's and he turned to face him, his face twisting into an angry roar.

"TAKE THEM!"

Isaac howled out a warning as Keith's army flooded into the clearing.

Serena pulled herself to her feet and fired an auric arrow into the skull of one of Keith's vampires as it hurled itself at her. "Nikki! You're up!"

Nikki smirked, her tattoos glowing brightly as she ducked below an enemy therion's swipe and drove the handle of one of her Sais into her attacker's windpipe. As the therion gasped and whimpered, staggering back and clutching its throat, she shouted to Zane; "Let them meet *Maledictus*!" She smirked, driving the point of her other Sai through the bottom of the gasping therion's jaw and let it spear through its skull before casting her magic and hurling its corpse into an oncoming group.

Zane bit his lip and glanced back at Serena as she fired two auric arrows through the chests of a pair of attackers and, using her hold on them, drove them into one another with bone-crushing force. As they collapsed in a broken heap she turned to Zane and nodded, "Do it!" She urged him, "Just leave Keith alive!"

Zane growled, "If I lose control of it and threaten the cause"—he grimaced and gasped as both of his arms twisted and shattered; stretching under their own weight until his fingers nearly met the frost-tinted turf—"you *need* to stop me, Serena!" His eyes bulged as another wave of agony hit him and he slammed into the ground as he began to pop and contort. "N-no ma-matterrrr... *what!*" he shrieked as the lower-half of his spine elongated with a wet crunch and left his upper torso sagging under the poor support, "*You... must... s-s-STOP—*" Zane's eyes went wide from pain and the words caught in his throat as his body seized and froze in mid-writhe. The battle paused for a moment—friend and foe alike craning to see what had happened—as his body went limp and sagged under its own heft before exploding into the beast's form and sneering. *"YOU WON'T STOP US!"*

Serena's eyes went wide as *Maledictus* rose to his full height and grabbed two of Keith's followers in his hands and scooped up another five in his aura. Dangling his captives high above him—forcing them to watch his activities—he began cackling as he crushed the first from the middle and then, tossing the still-dying vampire aside, twisting the other's limbs free of his joints one-by-one until he finally grew tired with him, as well, and pulled his head off like a doll's.

Serena watched this for a moment, chuckling at the child-like exuberance in the midst of his "play" before turning away and returning her focus to the battle.

Nikki smirked as she leapt over a towering therion, driving her Sais into its shoulders and cartwheeling over its head as her tattoos flashed and the pale-white magic crushed its skull; splattering a layer of gore across her face like war paint as she landed on the other side. "You think he's having fun, Serena?"

Serena laughed, "I do! I was actually starting to get jealous!" She punctuated her last word by firing an auric bow into the chest of an approaching freak as she shook her head. A *freak*! Keith—Mister High and mighty Council-supporter—had been turning humans into raving, psychopathic, deranged third-generation vampires solely to build up his army. That was something, which, in and of itself, was *at least* three broken laws punishable by execution and *multiplied* by each and every ravenous Mythos mishap she saw thrashing about.

Shrieking at the auric arrow in its chest, the freak foamed at the mouth and began to charge at her still. Sighing, she shook her head and began expanding it inside him, causing his upper torso to burst and leaving his legs to kick about in momentary confusion.

Nikki laughed at Serena's show and nodded her approval

before shifting her focus to her left, "Isaac! Cover the flank!"

Nodding his foxlike head, Isaac barked and snarled, gesturing to the other therions from his pack and directing them into battle around the edge of the clearing before charging forward on all fours and jumping into a pod of enemies head-on. As the unsuspecting sang in the middle was speared by Isaac's dive into them, the others spilled in either direction like bowling pins from the impact. Before they'd had a chance to hit the ground, Isaac had already torn his enemy's throat out and, spitting the bloody wad from his mouth, stood to his full height and backhanded the nearest vampire before starting in on the others.

"Zoey, check his blind-side!" Nikki called as she threw a Sai into an enemy's chest before drawing it back to her with her magic.

Darting and weaving like a dancer between enemy attacks and letting her bubbly blue aura do the dirty work as she put each of Keith's followers behind her, Zoey closed-in on Isaac like a Hell-born ballerina—leaving a trail of headless foes behind her—and leaping gracefully into the air and pulling Isaac off the ground and out of the path of several enemy therions.

Isaac's animal eyes widened for a moment as he floated over the battlefield before coming to rest and beamed over at Zoey, who nodded—blowing him a kiss—before letting him drop down onto the confused Mythos below for the slaughter.

Nikki continued to bob-and-weave like a glowing ninja while shouting commands to the others around her. As Serena watched, the efforts of their small band of fighters began to open a pocket in the middle of the clearing that left Serena, *Maledictus*, and Keith to handle their end.

"Why do you"—*Maledictus* sang in his multilayered, gravelly voice—*"build us up, butter-cup baby,"* he hurled one of the last four Mythos he'd been playing with nearly one-hundred feet into the air, as his aura lashed out behind him and began pulling another's limbs off before dropping them—crippled and useless—to the ground to bleed to death, *"Just to let us down?"* He smirked as he threw out his hand and caught the still-shrieking airborne Mythos

and holding them to his face as he sneered, *"And mess us around! And **worst** of all…"* The vampire let out one final cry only to have it cut short as *Maledictus* drove his forehead into his face and caved it in. Pouting playfully at the gory remnants of his enemy's face, *Maledictus* shook his head, *"… you **never** call, baby, when you say you will."*

Raising an eyebrow, Serena shook her head and chuckled, "Hey! You almost done?"

Maledictus looked up at her and smirked, tossing aside the corpse and stepping towards her as he finished his song, *"But we love you still!"*

Serena shook her head at him, "Even as a killing machine you're a smooth talker."

"Only for you, buttercup baby!" His enormous grin widened as his scarlet aura whipped about around him. Stepping beside her, he shifted his eyes towards Keith, who had watched—wide-eyed and unbelieving—at the scene around him. *"Let us break him!"* He looked pleadingly at Serena, *"Just this once! We WANT to see him inside-**out**!"*

"I know you do, baby," Serena patted his shoulder, "but there's far worse in store for him."

Maledictus scoffed, *"There is NOTHING worse than US!"*

Serena smirked, "I know, sweetie, but others want to play with him, too."

The playful conversation between them seemed to shake Keith from his horrified stupor and he narrowed his eyes at them. "Fine! If *that's* how it has to be!" He wrapped his fists in his aura, "Then who am I to disappoint?"

Maledictus rolled his shoulders and stretched his neck, *"Can we break his legs? No killing—we promise—just fracture his **fucking** femurs!"*

Serena frowned, glaring at Keith and shaking her head, "No, baby. I think I want to do this one on my own."

A disappointed whimper emerged from *Maledictus'* throat, but he did nothing to protest as Serena stepped forward.

"Admirable move," Keith started towards her, nodding,

"*Stupid*, but admirable, nonetheless."

"We'll see," she sneered, letting her auric bow appear in her hand.

She glared and let out a loud cry and began firing a series of auric arrows as she rushed towards Keith.

"Ah-hah! *There's* the brash bitch we know and love!" Keith sprinted at her, ducking and rolling around every auric strike that came at him and drawing nearer.

Serena roared, firing more and more auric bolts at him until their source became a violet blur in her hands, but no matter how many she threw or how fast she threw them, Keith evaded and continued towards her.

"Did you *forget*, Serena? Have all our years taught you *nothing*?" He jumped over a wave of bolts and continued at her, "I have *always* had the upper hand! I'm faster! I'm stronger! And I'm *smarter*!" Keith grinned and focused his aura into his right hand, elongating it into an auric blade, "And I know *all* your tricks!"

Serena fired an auric bolt at his feet and he side-stepped to avoid the explosion of turf, "You want to talk about *forgetting*, Keith?" She fired another wave of auric bolts that forced Keith to redirect his approach and come in from her right, "How 'bout we talk about forgetting your roots?" She fired more at his feet and forced him into the air before slamming an auric shot into his chest and throwing him to the ground.

Growling, he pulled himself up and started in at her again, "I'll see you *tortured* for that!"

"How about we discuss forgetting your place?" She shot into overdrive and repositioned herself several yards away, once again forcing him to recalculate his approach. She sent another set of arrows at him that he easily evaded, "Or how about we get personal, Keith! Like when you forgot which fork to use at Dad's big dinner with the Keilano Clan leader and you threw a hissy fit and shit your pants?" She laughed and fired directly at his chest, only to arc back around once he'd dodged it to knock him to his side. "Or that time you forgot to wear a belt at that ball in Venice and I pulled down your pants in front of the ambassador's daughter?" she cackled, sending more auric bolts at him and beginning to clip him in his efforts to get to her. "Did you *forget*, dear brother, just how unimpressed she was with what she saw?"

"Shut up! Shut-the-fuck-up!" he roared, throwing out another auric blade in his left hand and leaping at her.

Before he could land she'd jumped into overdrive and put another hundred yards between them. "Funny that you accuse me of forgetting when you've clearly allowed so much to slip your mind. You see"—she fired more arrows and succeeded in knocking him down once again—"you *are* faster, and you're *definitely* stronger!" She smirked as she hooked another auric bolt around and pulled his feet out from under him and cackled at his rage-fueled roar. Throwing out his aura, he pushed himself off the ground and charged at her again. Serena shook her head, sneering, "But I'm beginning to second-guess that *smarter* thing."

Keith jumped at her and swung with his auric blade, nearly taking her arm off as she rolled free, "Oh? Would you care to elaborate?" he growled.

Serena giggled, "Well, for starters, I have to question the sort of mind that can allow a man to forget what his dick is for!" She ducked under another strike and shifted behind him, "Or how you can find reason to boast when you have the body of an eight year old girl! But, more than *anything* else, Keith, I think you're a dumb-fuck because you've forgotten that I've always been better than you at *one* thing!"

He glared and turned to strike, "And what would *that* be?" He growled and overshot the attack, only to have Serena drive her knee into his groin.

Serena howled in laughter as he hissed in pain, his aura whipping about in a fit of rage. "See? You're dumb ass has already forgotten!"

"You can't do *anything*!" He lunged and missed again.

"Nope," she smirked at him, "You forgot that I could *always* piss you of—"

Keith roared in triumph as he brought his auric blade around and stabbed right through her abdomen. Serena gasped as blood dripped down her chin from the attack and pulled back, staring down at the gaping hole in her stomach. The battlefield went deathly quiet as she dropped to her knees and looked up at her still-heaving brother with fading eyes.

"S-see?" she coughed and struggled to smile, "Y-y-you... you did forget..."

Keith shook his head, "I have *never* forgotten how much you piss me off, Serena! And I think now you'll remember that!"

Serena groaned and inhaled sharply, nodding, "Perhaps. But you d-did forget"—she coughed up some more blood and groaned—"t-two *very* im-important... things."

He smirked and knelt down, "Do tell. What have I forgotten?"

"You weren't... su-supposed..." She grimaced and threw out her hand to catch her as she started to fall to the ground, "... to kill a member of Vail... without Council consent..."

Keith's eyes widened as his rage-clouded vision shifted to reveal his mistake and he began to shake.

"And..." Serena chuckled, "... you forgot... about... him," she managed to point over her brother's shoulder at *Maledictus* before her strength left her and she hit the ground.

CHAPTER SIXTEEN
JUST US

NIKKI'S EYES WIDENED AS SHE ran towards *Maledictus*. The beast had gone berserk with rage after watching Keith stab Serena, and while she was worried for the sake of her friend's wellbeing— Serena's usually bold and vibrant purple aura rapidly fading—it was, as much as she hated to admit it, Keith that she was most concerned for.

If he died now, everything they'd just accomplished would be for nothing.

"*Maledictus*! You *must not* kill him!" She yelled, her tattoos flaring as she tried to calm the curse. Though the speed and ferocity diminished from the monster's attacks, it did not stop them. "Help Serena! *Maledictus*, you *can* save her!"

This stopped the onslaught for a moment—the half of Keith's face that wasn't hemorrhaging and swollen beyond use gazing out thankfully for a pause in the rampage—and the rage-filled face of Zane's curse turned away from its work to snarl at her:

"WE DO NOT SAVE! WE ARE DEATH! WE ARE DESTRUCTION!" He jabbed a finger at Keith, causing the beaten and bloodied vampire to wince, *"AND WE WILL NOT STOP UNTIL HE IS—"*

Nikki, now beside him, brought her hand down on the beast's face, "Shut the hell up and keep Serena alive!"

Maledictus snarled and narrowed his eyes at Nikki as he raised a massive clawed hand.

Nikki narrowed her eyes, her tattoos flaring, *"If* you care about her you'll be able to *stop* killing and destroying for *five* minutes!" The scarlet aura and fiery rage in *Maledictus'* eyes calmed and shifted to Serena. "That's what I thought," Nikki nodded, "Now do whatever you can for her!"

As it turned out, the *Maledictus* curse—one that was created to kill, maim, torture, mutilate, and destroy—made the curse surprisingly good at knowing how to treat the conditions of its handiwork. Unable to focus entirely on the task of keeping Keith's ravaged body from slipping into unconsciousness, Nikki found herself glancing back at the beast as its scarlet aura worked fervently on keeping Serena's vitals stable. Zoey, after helping Isaac and the others finish off those of Keith's army who hadn't fled into the woods after *Maledictus* had begun painting the clearing with him, had hesitantly stepped beside the strangely calm beast to do anything she could for her friend, though the assistance seemed unnecessary at that point. Stealing another glance, Nikki watched again as *Maledictus* utilized its knowledge of anatomy and pain tolerance to numb Serena's agony while keeping her life-force from fading any further than it already had.

She bit her lip and turned back to Keith, throwing another wave of magic into his body to keep his heart beating and hoping the impact hurt him.

It just seemed so… unnatural.

As dawn approached and the sun began to take its scheduled journey over the horizon, a roar of vehicles grew in the distance. Being so deep in the forest, the sound of anything motorized— short of the occasional dirt-bike or four-wheeler driven by thrill- seeking campers—was an alien one, and as every ear in the clearing still attached to a living brain was made aware of it, all attention turned towards it.

When the first of the pitch-black SUVs broke through the brush and into the clearing—kicking up clumps of frosted earth under its belted tires—and skidded to a violent stop, it became very evident that campers were not the source.

This Jeep was soon after joined by several others that were just as dark and tinted and ominous, and as they came to stop around the first their doors swung open simultaneously and a team of Mythos in equally dark suits stepped out. With nearly three dozen seemingly identical figures strategically placing themselves around the clearing—some casting out their auras in preparation for whatever might be stupid enough to try something while others kept their hands close to whatever gun or bladed weapon they'd strapped to their waist—and making sure that anything that *could* surprise them would be unable to. After a moment, one of the aurics that had stayed nearer to the parked caravan reached out with a pine-green aura to each of the others and took a psychic reading before giving a final sweep of the clearing and nodding to somebody in the back of the center SUV.

As the door opened, the clearing went ten degrees colder. With every eye glued to him, an immaculate vampire with slicked-back blonde hair and a finely-trimmed, matching goatee and sporting a blood-red three-piece suit stepped out and nodded to the auric.

"Thank you, Angelo. If you and the others can begin to tidy up I'd like to have a moment alone with our new friends."

The auric nodded and quietly turned, gesturing to the others. In a flash of activity, the sangs in the group vanished into overdrive and the aurics began a choreographed sweep of the area with their auras. In less than ten seconds, nearly all of the dead bodies had vanished and all evidence of the battle stripped from the landscape.

"So graceful..." Zoey stared in awe.

"Aren't they, though?" the blonde vampire chimed in a smooth Italian accent as he stepped towards them, beaming a perfectly-white smile beneath a pair of perfect green eyes. "It's always fun to watch them work," he quirked an eyebrow at the sight of *Maledictus* and lingered on Serena's body before moving his gaze as he took in each of them. "What? Why's everyone so tense? Oh my, of course! Where are my manners?" He bowed slightly, "My name is Damiano Moratti—fifth chair of The Council—and I've come in regards to a troubling message from Vail-heiress, Serena."

Zoey frowned, looking down at Serena for a moment, "Troubling?" She frowned at Damiano, "What do you mean? When did she—"

"I believe her *exact* words were..." He frowned and shook his head, reaching into the breast pocket of his coat and pulling out a small piece of parchment, "Ah yes! 'Incompetent sheep-fuckers'— so delightfully charming, yes?" He glanced at the leering *Maledictus* and nodded, "You have a keeper, my friend!"

Maledictus sneered and stifled a growl.

"Down, Dino. We're here to help," he waved a condescending hand at the beast as he turned his back on him and started towards Keith. "Yes, *quite* troubling indeed. I daresay that for one to use such"—he smirked—"*colorful* language when addressing us is a sign that things *may* have gotten out of hand somewhere." He knelt down in front of Keith, rubbing the flat of his thumb against the bottom of his goatee, "Wouldn't you say so, *compagno*?"

Keith whimpered and groaned in pain as he tried to put distance between himself and Damiano and forgetting that *Maledictus* had, true to his word, fractured both of his femurs. The tremor of pain and ensuing threat of shock reminded Nikki that she had stopped casting on him when The Council had arrived, and she went to give Keith another dose of magic.

"Oh no no no, *bella*, that will not be necessary. From what I've gathered on my way here our dear Keith is *quite* capable at taking care of matters himself." His green eyes shifted for the first time to something terrifying and the air chilled-over once again in response as he shifted his dagger-like gaze back at Keith, "Isn't that right?"

Keith shook his head, trying to form words with a broken jaw but only succeeded in offering an airy whistle as it passed through the series of broken teeth in his mouth.

Damiano stood and folded his arms behind his back, nodding to Nikki, "You've done beautifully, my dear, but we'll take it from here." He sighed, shaking his head, "I must say, Vailean, I'd *wanted* to like you—this is not to say that I ever *did*—since your father *was* held in such high regards with us. However, to be perfectly honest, I and many of the other chairs found you to be something of a nuisance" He shook his head, "When Gregori refused the offered chair that you so enthusiastically volunteered for, we were, though disappointed at his decision, hopeful that you—of his own *blood*— would serve to some adequate respect in his honor."

Zoey and *Maledictus* stared at Damiano in awe.

Gregori had been offered a chair with The Council?

"However, as we'd feared, *honor* is not something you'd know too much about, and while we would have liked nothing better than to see you serve as a feeder, we *do* have an etiquette to abide by," he shook his head at that, "And, with no reason to bleed you like a wine grape, there was nothing we could do." He sneered and reached out with his bright yellow aura and pulled Keith to his full height—keeping his toes an inch above the ground—and keeping him conscious despite the growing pain, "'Incompetent sheep-fuckers' indeed. You have, to say the least, *disappointed* us, Keith, and, as you will come to find out over the next few months of your sentence, we do not take well to disappointment. This will perhaps go without saying, but you *are* aware of our affinity for protocol." He nodded to several aurics that had been waiting nearby and glared at Keith as they stepped forward and wrapped him in a reinforced, auric-blocking straightjacket. Thrashing and groaning, they pulled his head back and held his mouth open as Damiano's aura reached out and tore his fangs from his gums. As the severed teeth slowly floated into the vampire's hand, the auric guards pushed Keith forward and slipped a metal guard over his bleeding mouth and, using a small drill that one of them drew from their pocket, drove several screws into his jaw to hold it in place to keep him from biting.

Damiano's posture straightened and his voice shifted to one of authority, "Keith Vailean, for your deceit against The Council and your crimes against the Mythos community I, Damiano Moratti—fifth chair of The Council—with the unanimous written-and-spoken consent of the other chairs, do place you under formal Council arrest. All rights and privileges bestowed by your superiors are hereby stricken and all benefits and protections offered by your comrades are hereby revoked. For the severity of your crimes you will be denied trial and bail and none, with the exception of the unanimous consent of all Council chairs, will be permitted to cease or alter the conditions of your punishment. Do you understand and acknowledge?"

Keith narrowed his eyes and let loose a series of muffled grunts and whines from behind his surgically-attached mask.

Damiano smirked and nodded, "I will take that as a 'yes'." He nodded to the aurics, "See that he's secured before you leave and be sure that there's a holding tank and a fully-equipped surgical team waiting for him in Rome; the others will want to put him on display immediately!" He glared at Keith as they dragged him away, "This will not be pleasant. I promise."

As Keith was dragged away by the aurics, Damiano adjusted his jacket and turned to the others, his bright smile and sunny demeanor suddenly returning. "Again, my friends, I thank you for calling this situation to our—"

"*Save her! WE KNOW YOU CAN!*" *Maledictus* growled as he stood and glared at him.

Nikki frowned, "*Maledictus!*"

"*Maledictus?*" Damiano smirked and nodded, "Ah yes! The *maledetto!* Gregori's warrior; the one with the Taroe curse, yes?" He nodded at the beast before him as though he approved, "Impressive. A tad excessive, I must say, but it has appeared to gotten the job done."

Maledictus snarled and bared his teeth, "*We will not let you leave until—*"

"I'm sorry, what was that?" Damiano took a step towards him and sneered, "You'll *let* us leave? Is that what I'm to gather from this exchange?" He shook his head, "No. *We* do not answer to the demands of *any*, and certainly not to those of violence made by those who *serve* us!"

Maledictus roared, "*WE SERVE NOONE!*"

Damiano smirked, "Then there's nothing to discuss," he turned to walk away.

Raving from the response, *Maledictus* lunged at the Italian vampire.

"*Maledictus!* No!" Nikki's eyes widened.

"Zane!" Zoey started forward but was thrown back by Damiano's yellow aura.

In a flash of movement and light, *Maledictus* was thrown off his feet and brought to his back; an auric bind fastening about his throat and tightening until his gasps were choked and rasped. As the beast's kicking feet were tethered in the same fashion, Damiano appeared over him. Catching *Maledictus'* arm in mid-swipe and breaking it over his knee, Damiano drove the heel of his foot into the beast's chest over its heart. As *Maledictus* cried out in agony, he wrapped him in his aura and immobilized his body as his right hand gripped him at the chin and began to drain his life-force.

Nikki shivered as the air went cold, staring in shock at the display.

"N-no!" Zoey whimpered.

Whimpering, *Maledictus'* body began to shift and deflate as he transformed back into Zane.

"P-p-please…" Zane whimpered, looking up at the Italian vampire. "Please don't let her die…"

Damiano frowned, glaring down at him. "If I extend to you this favor—*if* I grant you your request—do you *swear* to The Council to control the thing inside you?"

Zane grimaced as the final steps of the transformation sent an agonized wave through his body. Stifling the cries of pain, he nodded, "Y-yes! I do! Just save her!"

Damiano smiled and stood, turning away from him and stepping over to Serena and bowing his head to Zoey, "If you'll pardon me, miss."

Zoey blushed and stepped aside.

Staring down at her, Damiano cocked his head, peering at the gaping wound in her stomach before letting his aura out and scanning her body for any other signs of damage. "*Tale dramma…*" He sighed, "Cursed-boy! Here!"

Zane groaned, still recovering from Damiano's beating, and hurried beside him, "Wh-what is it? Will she—"

"You love the girl, yes?"

Zane stared, stunned, "I… I do, yes."

Damiano nodded, "That would explain the idiocy."

Zane bit his lip, "What do you—"

A sharp slap connected with the back of Zane's head, "Blood! The girl needs blood! Idiot!" Damiano shook his head, "If you can't use your *brain* for her, at least open a vein for her!"

"She…" Zane looked down at Serena, "She's going to be okay?"

Damiano sighed, "Not if you keep whimpering over her like an idiot! Will you give the girl what she needs and stop waiting for the forest to break out into song? Idiot! This is not a cartoon!" He stood and turned, "And this doesn't change our agreement, boy.

Just because you're an idiot doesn't make me a fool!"

Zane blushed, quickly biting into his wrist and beginning to feed it to Serena. At first the flow merely welled in her mouth, the excess beginning to spill past her parted lips and rolling down her cheek. As the crimson trail reached a vertical drop from her jaw, it began a steady drip to the ground and Zane started to turn so that he could call to Damiano to return.

A choked gurgle sounded from Serena and the blood in her mouth was abruptly swallowed before she heaved and her eyes shot open, "N-need more!"

"Serena?" Zane turned to her.

Serena coughed and licked some of the blood from her lips, "The one and only, baby." Her breathing began to steady as she lifted her purple eyes to Zane's wide and disbelieving own. "So… did we win?"

Zane, despite the situation, couldn't hold back the laugh. "Yea, hon. We won. Keith's on his way to being a Mythos Pay-Per-View torture special."

"Oh good," Serena sat up, grimacing as her still-healing stomach was forced to work, "I hope they put a cherry-bomb up his ass. Come to think of it, that sounds too—"

"SERENA!" Zoey's shrill voice chimed a split second before she collided with her, "GLOMP!"

"Ow! Bitch!" Serena groaned as she was knocked over under the playful assault, "New rule; abdominal wound CLOSED before GLOMPING ensues!"

Zoey giggled, "Deal!"

Nikki smiled as she stepped over, "Okay! I've gotten things all patched up with The Council." She glanced at Zane before addressing the others, "They said that, while they have to keep a watch on all Vail activity for the next few months—'protocol' as Damiano put it—it looks like you're all otherwise in the clear."

Serena frowned, noticing the way she watched Zane with envy in her eyes and bit her lip. This girl had some sort of attachment to Zane that she couldn't place. Though she could see it wasn't love, it certainly wasn't hate, either.

She knew that her being a Taroe already made her on Zane's bad side. She wanted to be nice to her though; she had brought Zane back to her before the fight. She smiled over at Nikki and nodded warmly.

"We should get back. She's right," she said.

"Will you be ok walking?" Zane looked down at her and after a second thought; he lifted her against him and began to walk through the forest back to their home.

"You don't need to carry me, Zane," Serena pouted and blushed, enjoying the feeling of his chest against her.

"You like it. Don't deny it," he smirked, his fangs extending as he looked at her. She could sense the attraction growing between them as they walked forward. She felt another blush creep up her cheeks and frowned. She was never this bashful against anyone before.

"You going to tie me to those train tracks yet, Snidely?" she smirked, the memory of their first meeting playing through her head.

"Only if you like it that way," he grinned.

CHAPTER SEVENTEEN
SETTLING

"DO YOU REMEMBER WHEN we first met?" Zane asked, staring at the ceiling of their underground base.

"Of course I do. How could I ever forget?" she answered, smirking, "I beat the shit out of you."

Laughing, he slapped a palm over his face and shook his head, "You know what? Nevermind. I don't think I want to finish this thought."

Serena giggled and shook her head, putting her hand on his chest, "No! You can't just leave me hanging like that!"

"Sure I can," he smirked. "What are you going to do about it?"

She glared, "I can beat the shit out of you *again*!" She jabbed him in the shoulder.

"Ow!" He looked over, "Oh *that's* it!" He laughed as he rolled on top of her and playfully pinned her down, smiling down at her as she giggled under his hold and he nodded, "Yea... you were just as stunning that night as you are now. Even in the beginning, even though I was such a hopeless dick, I saw something in you."

"But, though I had felt something even then, I knew—I could just *tell*—you were desperately in love with someone else. That night, when Devon took my body so that he could have you, I watched you from the back of my own mind—sharing the view with the beast as we both watched you and fell for you—and the emotions and passion and energy in your face gave us hope that, maybe, neither of us had to live as what we were expected to; I didn't have to be the cursed jerk waiting to fade away. But then, after all was said and done, I was afraid. Though I didn't fight it—I mean, how could I?—I still knew I had no chance. But, now he's gone and it's just me and..." Zane sighed and frowned, "Serena, I want you to know that... fuck! I don't know how to say this!"

"Zane...what are you trying to say? You're rambling." She frowned, "What is it? You know you can tell me anything."

Zane frowned and looked over at her as she ran her left hand over his face for a moment. As she smiled and withdrew her hand, he spotted the glistening ring that she wore on her left hand— Devon's ring—and narrowed his eyes at it. He knew she was over her long-dead lover and had moved on, but seeing the wedding band still wrapped around the ring finger of her left hand made him think that maybe she wasn't ready for what he had in mind. Sighing, he forced a smile and kissed her hand.

"I just... I never thought I'd be in this position. I never thought anything would change for me. And, though I know you can step out into the world and have *anybody* you set your eyes on, I just wanted to tell you that I won't ever have eyes for anyone else. I love you, Serena."

Serena blushed, staring at him for a long moment—her eyes shimmering as they read the sincerity in his face—before she leaned her head against his strong chest and sighed softly.

"Zane..." She whispered and lifted her head to his, "... I would *never* want to see somebody else the way I see you. No matter what you think you know, I do—and I always will—love you."

Feeling a well of happiness, he smiled and gingerly pressed his lips to hers.

Holding the kiss for a long, tender moment, Serena slowly parted his lips with her tongue and capturing his mouth completely with her own. As his tongue met hers, he felt a flash of heat and in the passion of the moment, he heard a growl but couldn't bring himself to care who it had come from.

His arms lifted as her hands moved quick, desperate to separate their bodies from their clothing. Their mouths parted momentarily to get their shirts off and pressed back, more passion growing between them. Without breaking the kiss, he peeled away her pants along with his and pushed himself over Serena on the bed and continued to kiss her as they once again became one.

Nothing else mattered at that moment.

It was simply Zane and Serena's world.

Zoey smiled and adjusted herself against Isaac's chest as they settled into bed, "You were so incredible today!"

Isaac smirked, "So were you," he rubbed his palm along her sides, "I had no idea you were such a great fighter!"

"I wasn't that great," Zoey blushed, "I just felt like I had to work harder because of everybody else."

"Well, either way, I've never seen anybody fight that way!" Isaac kissed the top of her head, "You were so graceful!"

"I owe a lot of that to Serena," Zoey confessed, "Seeing her grow and learn over the past few days really gave me something to aspire to." She smiled, "She's gotten stronger since I first met her. A lot stronger!"

"I bet. You and Zane are certainly great teachers, but..." He bit his lip and looked down.

"But what?" Zoey looked up.

"I was just wondering if you think she's ready for what she's taking on. I mean, I agree that she's strong and everything, but is that going to be enough to rebuild her father's clan *and* become their leader?" Isaac sighed as he looked down at her nervously, "I don't mean to be rude, but she hasn't had to do *anything* like this. I've only had to lead the small pack of therions in the woods and *that's* challenging enough."

Zoey moved closer to her lover and sighed, leaning her head on his shoulder. Her short, blue, pixie styled hair fell over her face, "I know what you mean, Isaac, and I understand your concern. But I have to be hopeful. She's Gregori's daughter, and I've seen too many incredible things from him to make a judgment just yet," she confessed, smiling up at him. "I know it's weird, but I have faith in her."

"That's enough for me," Isaac admitted. "And besides, since she agreed to rebuild with my pack as members I'll be happy to help in any way I can," he smiled.

Zoey smiled back, "It means a lot to me to know that we'll be clan-mate's and that we'll have a chance to rebuild like this. It's going to be great!" She turned to Isaac and leaned closer, catching his lips in hers and simply relishing in the moment of being in Isaac's embrace.

Nikki sighed as she sat in the forest, watching the moon from the clearing that, only hours earlier, she and the others had battled so ferociously in. Her emotions had overwhelmed her and had wrecked her mind and she needed a break.

It was just too tolling to be *that* close to him and not be able to do anything about it.

She had finally allowed herself to see him again and, though she had known it was the wrong approach, she hadn't been able to help herself. Though she couldn't even be sure if she was wasting her time or not, seeing Zane's face back at the tribe's land had been too much of an opportunity to let pass. She *had* to know the truth! Though she hadn't been completely honest with him when she first saw Zane, she'd known it had been him that she was looking for and, she wouldn't have been able to figure out where to even start. Staring at the sky and letting out a deep sigh, she allowed herself to close her eyes as the memories built within her.

It was all driving her insane!

She'd just been missing him so much and, ever since she'd lost him all those years back, she'd been traveling alone and taking on any odd job that presented itself to her in whatever no-name town she'd happened across. And, while each new "home" was effective in helping her help clear her thoughts for a time, the pain of her memories never failed to find her time and time again. It was becoming all-too clear that she would never be able to move on without some sense of closure.

Like it or not, she *had* to know the truth.

After all, he had been the *only* one who could stop her suffering in the past, and if there was *any* hope—any chance that she could find some way to have him back or to at least find closure to his absence—then she was determined to find it.

She frowned, looking up into the sky.

She had to go back to the clan.

CHAPTER EIGHTEEN
DEADLY REUNION

"HEY ZANE?"

Silence.

Serena frowned and rolled over, leaning her head on his shoulder as he continued to stare up into the canopy of starlight as it cut through the openings in the treetop's canopy. "Zane? Is everything alright?"

Zane's eyes shifted slowly from one constellation to the next as whatever was haunting his thoughts kept him distracted and staring off into the distance.

Whatever it was, it looked like he was upset by it.

Biting her lip, Serena sat up and nudged him in the ribs, "Hey! Earth-to-vacant-eyed Zane!"

He blinked and finally turned his attention to her, realizing that he'd been zoning out and frowned. He was making her worry and he didn't mean for that. Their path towards rebuilding their lives was just beginning and, though this was a happy and prosperous chance for all of them, he couldn't help but worry about what could possibly go wrong.

After all, The Council was keeping tabs on all of them now, and they were sure to put a stop to anything and everything they saw as a threat.

"I'm sorry, Serena. I was just thinking," Zane answered finally.

"Really? I hadn't noticed! I just thought you were *ignoring* me because you never wanted to see me naked again!" She stuck out her tongue and rolled her eyes, "You want to tell me what's the matter?"

Zane sighed and shrugged, "I'm just nervous about rebuilding. I don't want to end like the Odin clan."

"I know," Serena bit her lip, remembering the stories, "But haven't you heard? The Stryker boy's been turning his own situation around since waking up to that nightmare." Serena smiled, "From what I hear he's ruffling a lot of feathers, so obviously he's not letting the Odin situation stop him!" She smirked and leaned back, staring up at the sky. "He *does* sound like he'd be interesting to meet!" She giggled.

Zane sneered and shook his head, "He sounds like a loose cannon, to me! I heard he went on some solo run in Maine and left a clusterfuck of a mess. Some obscene number of human casualties left in the woods. Apparently The Council was cleaning up after his little camping trip for nearly two weeks!" Zane turned away, growling, "Must be nice to carry the Stryker name like that!"

"Oh? You mean like how I get to carry the Vailean name?"

Zane scoffed, "Hardly!"

"Aw! I think somebody's jealous," Serena chuckled, winking, "Afraid I'm gonna hop the Stryker boy if I got the chance?"

Zane sneered and turned back to her, "Like he could *handle* you!" He laughed and rested his head in Serena's lap, finally feeling relaxed in her presence.

With the fear of Keith destroying all of Gregori's hard work behind them, and the impending threat of execution from an angry Council fading like a bad memory, the only *real* threat wasn't in what was, but only what could be.

Serena smiled as she thought of how, in only a short time, she'd gone from living day-by-day in uncertainty and loneliness to having an epic new chapter in not only her life, but in the lives of all those in her new clan; a clan that she would be overseeing with Zane by her side. Blushing at the thought, she gazed down into his gloriously mismatched eyes and ran her hand across his cheek.

"I love you so much, Zane."

Zane blushed, "I'll never get tired of hearing that."

Serena nodded and smiled, "And I'll never get tired of saying it." She laughed and nodded, looking over at Zane for a moment. Her smile broadened as his gaze bore into her. "I was wondering…"

"Hmm?" Zane looked over at her, "What is it?"

"Well, I was thinking: if I'm going to be in charge and whatnot, I should probably have a—" her eyes widened and she turned suddenly as a wave of dark blue auric energy approached. "No…" Her purple aura flared angrily as she shot to her feet as she shrieked in rage, "You?"

Zane frowned, not understanding her sudden outburst but standing up beside her, "Serena? What is it? What are you—"

Kristine's aura broke through the darkness as she strolled towards them, "I heard you'd dragged your bitch-ass out of whatever shit-hole you'd been squatting in, slut! And I *know* you weren't about to forget about what you did to us!"

Serena hissed, "Us? '*Us*'? Are you *insane!*"

Zane frowned and looked from the strange newcomer to Serena, "How do you know this…?" He paused as Serena sprinted by, charging at her.

"I'll fucking *kill* you!"

Kristine shook her head, "Not before I kill you, bitch! And *not* before I take him back!" Her purple aura seized and withdrew into her body, causing Serena to pause and backtrack.

"Wh-what? You're an auric? But... you and Devon... were *hunters*! H-how could you *hunt* vampires if..."

"You stupid bitch! *You* of all people should understand! I *knew* he wouldn't have me if he knew what I was, and cutting a few of our kinds' heads off to try and bag him was *more* than a fair trade, wouldn't you agree? But that's ancient history and I want him!"

Serena frowned, "What are you—"

"Devon, you stupid bitch!" Kristine shrieked, "I *know* he's with you! I *saw* him fuse with your aura the night you killed him and I want him—"

"*I* killed him?" Serena lunged at her, only to be thrown back as the auric threw out a wave of energy.

Kristine sneered, walking towards her, "*Where* is he?"

"He's gone." Serena glared, pulling herself up.

"Don't lie to me!" Kristine hissed, "I've come too far for that!"

Serena frowned, "It's not a lie, you *psycho-bit*—" she was cut off as she was forced to dodge another auric blast from Kristine and cried out as one hit her in the leg and dropped her to the ground.

"Serena!" Zane glared and turned to Kristine, his tattoos beginning to glow as his body started to shift.

"This doesn't concern you!" Kristine glared at him, charging for another attack.

Serena's eyes widened, "No! Leave him alone!"

"Oh?" Kristine looked at her, "Might this be a *new* love? Serena... *two* men at once? I mean, I *knew* you were a tramp, but—"

"I already told you; Devon's *dead*!"

Kristine shook her head, "*If* that's true, then I *owe* you for taking Devon from me!"

"You're crazy!" Serena stood, "*You* started that fire at our weddi—"

"*NO!*" Kristine glared, "Devon would've *never* married you! It was all you! All your fault!" She glared at Zane, "And I *will* take what I'm owed!" She smirked as she threw out her aura at Zane.

Serena's eyes widened as the blast hit Zane, "No!" She ran towards him as he slammed into the ground, "Oh god! Please no! Not again!"

But his aura was already gone.

His tattoos; cold and black.

His body...still.

Dead.

"Turn around, bitch! I'm not done with you, yet!" Kristine said, her soft steps approaching behind Serena.

Serena dropped to her knees, tears welling in her eyes, "Zane..."

Kristine's aura slammed into her back, knocking her to the ground. "Don't think I'll kill you so easy! I've waited too long for this! Now *turn around!*"

Serena sobbed, trying to suck in a breath through her aching lungs as she clenched her eyes.

"Zane... no, please! Please don't let it be true..."

Kristine grabbed her shoulder, "Turn arou—"

"Would you mind terribly if I asked you to try that once more?"

Serena looked down to meet dark brown eyes on Zane's face.

Serena blushed as she saw Zane stand and, after dusting himself off, look at his hands and smirk.

"Z-Zane?"

He didn't respond but, instead, smirked at Kristine and took a step towards her, "Oye! You hear me, girlie? I said I want you to attack me!"

Kristine frowned, "No... you're not you. You can't be..."

Serena bit her lip as a bright green aura shimmered and grew from his body, writhing and bubbling into life.

Serena struggled to her feet, starting towards him, "Zane!" Frowning, he shifted his dark eyes to hers for the first time and took her in absently, "I'm afraid not, luv. Not anymore, at least."

PREVIEW TO

MEGAN J. PARKER

Scarlet Dawn

"SERENA?" A FAMILIAR VOICE caressed her skin with ghostly warmth and she opened her eyes as was met with Zane's mismatched gaze.

"Zane?" She frowned, biting her lip, "How are…?"

"Serena… I miss you. I miss you so fucking much," Zane frowned, sitting on the edge of the bed.

Serena sat up, still not sure what she was seeing.

Was she dreaming?

His form was hazy and seemed to be lit by his own personal source; the strange, white glow faded in-and-out over his face.

"I… I miss you too, Zane! I swear I'll find you soon! I swear! I've never stopped looking! Once I find that bitch, she's dead; she's fucking dead!" Serena whimpered, crawling to the end of the bed to join the spectral shadow of her lover, "I won't rest until I've found her."

"I know you won't, babes; even if I told you to move on and be—"

"No! I'm not giving up on finding you!" Serena choked on a sob.

Zane smirked and nodded, "See? Just as stubborn as ever!"

"Zane…" Serena felt a rock lodge in her throat and her eyes began to burn.

"Shhh. It's going to be alright," his voice was calm and a wave
a reassurance rode on his words and rolled through her body.

She welcomed the feeling.

It *was* him!

Though she had no idea *how* he was there, this was all the
evidence she needed that he was still alive.

That she wasn't crazy to still be looking for him!

"I've been at such a loss without you," she felt the first few
tears roll over her eyes. "You goddam asshole! I'm not supposed to
cry like this…"

The warmth and affection in Zane's eyes did not sway.
"Don't worry. I won't tell anybody."

Serena laughed and clenched her jaw when she had enough
control to do so, bringing her fist down on the bed. "Dammit!
That's what I mean! I… I can't even stay *sad* with you there as…
as…" She shook her head, "Dammit, Zane, what's happened to
you? Where are you? Please… *Please* tell me where you are!"

Zane frowned and shook his head, "I'm… I'm not sure. It
doesn't feel like a *where*; most of the time I'm not even self-aware
enough to know *who* I am! Something just… something called to
me now. I suddenly saw a path and knew that you'd be at the end
of it." He shrugged and looked at his hands, moving as though he
was about to clap and instead letting one hand pass through the
other, "I actually *feel* like a projection of myself," he looked back up
at her, "but it's worth it if it means I can see you right now."

Serena whimpered and shook her head, "It just… nothing
feels the same anymore. I try—I swear I try—but I just feel so
hollow and tired. I always feel so weak lately."

"Well, that's your first mistake! Come on, Serena," Zane's
face widened as he grinned. "You weak? This coming from the
cold-hearted bitch who beat the shit out of me less than two
minutes after we first met? And now you're going to let *this* set you
back?" He cocked his brow, "The girl who'd blatantly ogled a
picture of a man in a Speedo *after* we'd just fucked like porn stars
feels lost without a single man? C'mon, babes, you could replace

me in the time it takes you to bat an eyelash."

Serena bit her lip, "I... I never meant any of those things, Zane," she looked down, "Even when I joke like that now I... I feel like there's a fist in my gut. I feel like I never got to show you how much I really cared; how much I *really* loved you."

Zane shrugged, "I'd say this is a decent start." He smiled, "Just don't let me forget it when I get back, okay?"

"I'll *never* let you forget it," Serena smiled. "Even when I'm kicking your ass for being a loser."

Zane chuckled and shook his head, "Still a hardcore bitch," he gave her one of his looks, "You *are* tough, Serena. You don't need anyone's reassurance."

"How can you be so sure of me?" Serena felt a sting in her lip and tasted blood. Despite this, she kept chewing on it.

Zane frowned at the sight and shook his head, "Because you're too stubborn and strong-willed to *ever* be *anybody's* bitch but your own. Believe in yourself." He leaned back, "So what's new anyway? Raith treating my body well?"

Serena shrugged, "I guess. He goes the gym a lot more than you ever did."

Zane chuckled, "You were all the workout I ever needed."

"Ah, well in that regard the body is going without," Serena quipped. "As much as it seems to rub Nikki the wrong way—or not at all, I suppose—I've been making sure of your ongoing celibacy."

"Ouch. All those years being locked in my head and Raith's cock-blocked the minute he's out in the open," Zane pouted. "Let the poor guy take a swing at Nikki. I'm sure they could both use it; not like it's me in there anyway."

"It's *your* body!" Serena glared.

"Said the girl who let her phantom boyfriend possess and date-rape me?"

Serena blushed, "That... that was different."

"Not sure how," Zane chided her. "If all of this body-slash-no-body shit has taught me *anything*, it's that love transcends the flesh. My body is in the other room—my flesh and blood and organ…"

Serena raised an eyebrow, "You only have *one* organ?"

Zane shrugged, "Only one that you *wouldn't* sell on the black market for a new car."

Serena nodded, "Fair enough."

Zane rolled his eyes. "The point is, my *body* is in there… but this part of me—this… spectral, airy nonsense—is what you're after; what's making you laugh and cry and beat the shit out of my three-thousand dollar mattress over."

Serena frowned and poked the mattress, "You paid three-grand for this?"

"*Maledictus* kept ripping up the cheap beds. Finally wrote a message in blood—though we never found out *whose*—on the walls of the main lobby that if we didn't upgrade then he'd destroy the city. Your father was pretty quick to special order that."

Serena sneered, "He always was a charmer. Not exactly missing him."

Zane looked over, "He hasn't emerged lately?"

"Not since…" Serena bit her lip.

"That son of a bitch probably only responds to *my* rage," Zane shook his head. "Those clever bastards!"

Serena frowned, "Who?"

Zane shook his head, "Don't worry about it. So how's the whole 'Clan Leader' role working out?"

Serena shook her head, "Like a jagged dump. The Council approved a new clan in town." She growled, "Bastards are coming in on *my* fucking turf."

"You tried pissing on a park tree yet? Y'know, if you're gonna play the whole 'mark your territory' game," Zane laughed.

"You're going to be a dick even like *this*?" Serena glared, "Don't think that just because I can't touch you I won't kick your ass!"

"Ha! There's the Serena I came to know and love! Good to see you are still in there," Zane smirked.

"There's nicer ways to console me. Just because a splinter in the balls is hilarious doesn't mean the laughter is the best medicine to fix it."

"Yeah, but you obviously don't love me for my manners. Just like I don't love you for your finishing school grades," he laughed, sticking his tongue at her. "So what do you plan to do with this clan?"

"I'm going to pay the assholes a little visit tomorrow. Show them not to fuck with me and all," she shrugged. "And I figured while I was visiting, I'd sneak around and see if I couldn't gather some intel on *exactly* why they've come to town."

"Oh? Why, do you think they're up to something?" He looked over.

"Because the Vail Clan's been an established force in this area for *decades*! Then, only a few short months after *I* yank the title of 'leader' from my dick-hole, power-hungry brother, The Council green-lights a totally new clan to build just downtown?" She shook her head, "This is in response to *something*, and there's no way it has nothing to do with me or what we've been doing."

"What you've been doing?"

Serena nodded, "Some small-time rogue rolled in to town last week and everyone seems to think *that's* what's motivating this response. A whole new clan for *one* rogue; that sound suspicious to you?"

"Yea, it really, really does actually," Zane frowned.

"What do you mean 'actually'?" Serena glared.

Zane shrugged, the pale glow over his ghostly form shifting and fading slightly, "Only that you're rarely that logical. At least on the surface, anyway." He shook his head, "Normally, The Council wouldn't waste resources for something like this; they'd just send one of their own if they felt the local clan was short-handed."

"That's exactly how I feel," Serena nodded, "but the others think it's normal and I should go say my introductions."

"You? Introductions?" Zane made a shuddering motion before turning back to her. "I'd like to see that!"

Serena blushed, "I… I wish you could see it, too"

"It's going to get better, Serena. You'll see," he smiled warmly and reached out to make a familiar motion. As his ghostly hand reached her chin, she raised her face to allow them both to believe he'd raised her face on his own. "Chin up, babes."

"Easy for you to say, phantom-Zane," Serena giggled.

"Oh you *know* I'm just as hot as the real thing," he stuck out his tongue and his body's glow began to fade again.

Serena bit her lip, "Unless I've finally gone crazy and you're just a figment of my imagination. Then you'd look however I'd want you to look."

"Nah, then I'd be here as Gerard Butler or Channing Tatum or one of those dry Hollywood queefs."

"See?" Serena cast an accusatory finger in his direction, "*That's* how *I'd* talk—though I'd *never* say an unkind word about my Tatum-tot…—anyway, that just proves that you *are* just a figment of my imagination!"

"Tatum…tot?" Zane shook his head, "Look, maybe we're just a pair of vulgar fucks who are too perfect for one another for the other to believe it could be real," he scoffed. "God damn… You're still as beautiful as I remember."

"O-kay. Now I know that was something my mind made you say!" Serena laughed, falling onto her back and staring at her ceiling. "This has been a nice crazy-bitch dream."

"Maybe. Maybe not," Zane shrugged it off and smirked over at her, "Either way, I'm enjoying it, too, so don't wake up just yet."

She felt her cheeks heat and sighed, "Even like this you can make me blush!"

"You know you love it," he grinned.

"Psh! How could I not?" She laughed, turning to him as she began to reach out, "I promise to find you soon."

"I'll be waiting. For as long as it takes," he smiled and moved his hand out to meet hers.

She wanted his warmth.

She wanted his touch.

She *needed* him.

As their palms met, Zane's hand rippled and phased through her skin, the ripple traveling up his arm. As she watched, his form weakened—the pale light fading—and he drifted off like vapor vanishing into the air, leaving Serena staring at the empty edge of her bed.

Alone...

She shivered and fell back into the only warmth she could turn to and pulled the blankets over her as she nuzzled her face into Zane's pillow.

His scent would continue to haunt her until she found him.

Whimpering, she finally allowed the tears to fall freely.

"Zane... you son of a bitch! Where are you?"

ABOUT THE AUTHOR

Megan J. Parker lives in upstate New York in a small town that is no easier to spell than it is to pronounce. She lives with her adoring fiancé, Nathan Squiers, and her two devil kitties, Trent and Yuki (don't let their innocent looks deceive you, they are devious little cats). Normally, she can be found with her face plastered to her MacBook Pro either designing a new book cover or writing/plotting her latest story.

On her down time, she likes reading and watching comedy or romantic movies. Her passion for telling stories is portrayed in all her work and when there's a story to tell, you can be sure she'll tell it to its full extent. She now is a co-owner for the up and coming publishing company, Tiger Dynasty Publishing, and is hoping to continue to expand this company to great lengths.